CAN YOU LEND A HAND?

A GRADUAL FEMINIZATION NOVEL

JENNIFER SWEET

❀ Created with Vellum

1

Earning a degree should be a celebratory time in one's life. The glitz and glamor of graduation day with students outside on the university quad, hurling their hats in the air as the Dean sends them off into the real world. Everyone's got jobs, partners, apartments... Sure it's freakin' terrifying to stare out at the void of adulthood and face it head-on, but there's beauty in that. I've been thinking about that lately... and how I'm experiencing the exact opposite of it.

While I have my cynical, negative days, I generally consider myself a positive person. I like to look forward, not backward, and I love the concept of helping people. In fact, it's probably why I pursued and succeeded in getting my Associate's Degree in Nursing. Yeah, yeah... I know, not a *doctor*... but everyone knows that nurses are the lifeblood of any medical setting. They take shit from both patients *and* doctors, holding down the fort from impending chaos. Plus, who the hell wants all that debt from medical school? And so that's exactly where I'm at today: I'm officially Anderson Saffron, ADN! Done and done!

But of course, it's never *really* that simple. To loosely quote Jeff Goldblum's Jurassic Park character, "Life finds a way... to *fuck things up.*"

I'm currently in a packed-to-the-brim Kia hatchback, driving from the suburbs of Chicago to the quirky, tourist trap town of Old Buffalo, Michigan. Why? Well, I guess my parents watched me graduate and were inspired to shake up their own lives as well. They sold their house (*my* childhood home), quit their jobs, and bought a condo in Puerto Rico. For a couple of boring suburbanites, this felt like an insane move. First of all, they've never even *been* to Puerto Rico. But mostly my parents have always been practical, level-headed people. I guess the itch for warmer weather and a fresh start at retirement was simply too irresistible.

Knowing I'm still without a job, they graciously offered to let me accompany them on their life-restart. Call me a sucker, but I decided to stick with the midwest... even if it means living in Southwestern Michigan with one of the oddest people on the planet: my mother's younger sister, Aunt Trinity.

You could fit everything I know about Aunt Trinity on a single index card. Despite being only a two hour drive away, she'd never been a real part of my life. Not for any malicious reason, but when you're so clearly the family oddball, you tend to forge your own path. From everything my Mom told me, she lives life on her own terms.

My phone dinged with around 15 minutes left in my trip,

cruising down an empty Red Arrow Highway. It was Aunt Trinity, sending what must be her third or fourth ever text to me.

'Please be quiet when you pull up so you don't disrupt filming. Thanks!'

Quiet? *Filming?* What the hell was she talking about? I had no idea what this lady even did for work — or *play*, for that matter — but I figured a simple thumbs-up emoji would suffice. I could pester her all I wanted once I arrived.

You'd think I'd have at least scouted out Old Buffalo before agreeing to spend the summer here, but you'd be wrong. Though at first glance, it at least seemed I hadn't *immediately* fucked up. The downtown was cute and quaint. Touristy, sure, but not in a Hollywood Boulevard gift-shop-every-ten-feet kind of way. The town had adorable cafés, grocery chains, and parks. At a stoplight, I noticed signs posted all around promoting upcoming fairs and community events. After all, even tourist towns need to cater to their locals.

Maybe calling it a tourist trap is an overstatement. From what my mother told me, Old Buffalo has three types of people: working class folks, wealthy lakeside land owners, and the tourists who rent houses *from* those wealthy lakeside owners. As my GPS led me closer to the lake and toward bigger homes, it was becoming clear that Aunt Trinity was indeed in the Old Buffalo upper class.

"54 Lumber Lane…" I muttered to myself as I peered at each passing house, scanning for a visible number. The estates were expansive and impressive, but in a completely different way from the Chicago suburbs. Lumber Lane — like many of these streets — was woodsy and shaded, and the houses around here seemed to embrace the natural, forest-like atmosphere. Many properties appeared to be hugged by nature itself — vines twisting and crawling on the walls, and bulky trees positioned out front like armored guards. It all seemed like such earthy overkill... but then again, you don't choose to live near a lake if you're not already a fan of nature.

I probably took longer than I should have doing my stalker-ish, slow drive-by of Aunt Trinity's neighbors, but I eventually came across a wooden stake at the intersection of the street and a gravel driveway that read '54 Lumber Lane.'

Aunt Trinity's house looked no more impressive than her neighbors — in fact, it was quite a bit smaller. But the house gave a Thomas Kincaid-like 'Cottagecore' energy that was certainly appealing. My hatchback banged and bumped down the long driveway while I gazed at the beautiful two-story colonial home immersed in a messy but tasteful array of colorful foliage. An old, wooden garage covered in chipped white paint stood to the left of the house. Whether intentional or not, Aunt Trinity's dark green Prius matched her estate perfectly.

The moment I parked I practically spilled out of the car, desperate to stretch my legs and explore my new home. But I abruptly remembered the warning text about Aunt Trinity's filming. I glanced around. Where *were* these cameras? I had no idea what to expect. Was this for work? For fun? Was she filming *me* as a prank? If it was some big production, nothing outside suggested it. The only way to find out was to gingerly approach the front door and hope I didn't mess up any takes. Aunt Trinity's wooden porch wasn't doing my stealthiness any favors, creaking with each step. But sure enough when I reached the front door, I peered inside and saw something *beyond* strange. No big cameras, no film crew, no costumes or big set pieces. Trinity was in the center of her living room — furniture shoved aside to the walls — and she was... *dancing*?

Well, 'dancing' is maybe giving her too much credit. It was more like a mix between a kickboxing routine and jumping jacks. But she was holding something tiny in her hand and spastically waving it in front of her body, all while making wacky faces. The whole scene was beyond bizarre.

Out of respect for her weird ritual, I simply waited at her front door, silently peering through the glass until she looked done. But it didn't take long. Only a minute went by and she was back on her phone. This seemed like my best chance. The front door was unlocked, so I gave it a little knock as I cracked it open.

"*Hey...* Aunt Trinity?" I called out, inching my way into the foyer. The interior was just as 'fairytale cottage-y' as the exterior. An old, woodsy feel with that hint of mystical, storybook charm. Even the grandfather clock to my immediate left was accented with metallic butterflies and surrounded by a smattering of house plants.

Aunt Trinity placed her phone on the table behind her and craned her neck to get a view of me. "Anderson? Hey!" The fit, petite woman trotted over to me and extended her arms for a big hug. Already I could tell she looked incredible for being in her early 40s. Full, long blonde hair pulled back into a ponytail, practically no wrinkles or signs of aging, and she was in-shape bordering on buff. Particularly for a woman. Hell, I'm only 20 and she looked just a few years older than me.

She pointed to her head. "Twins!" she shouted.

I stood there for a moment, confused until I realized she was referring to our matching ponytails. Though maybe 'matching' is a step too far. Her blonde hair was luscious and full while my mousy brunette hair, though *long*, was pretty limp and lifeless.

Nonetheless, I smiled warmly. Of course I had to remind myself that despite the blood connection, I was essentially hugging a stranger.

"Ah! I *SO* couldn't wait for you to get here. I love having guests!"

"Even this long-term?" I chuckled, hoping she wouldn't recant the gesture.

Aunt Trinity tenderly clutched my shoulder. "Anything for family."

That sentiment felt a little misplaced coming from a family member I never really knew, but I took her word for it. Hell, who was I to deny free housing for the summer?

"So, uh, Aunt Trinity…"

She stopped me and shook her head. "Please, just 'Trinity' is fine. We're both adults."

"Uh, okay. *Trinity*… not to be a snoop, but I noticed you, uh, *dancing* alone in the living room? Is that what you were filming?"

She paused, as if my questioning of her odd behavior was itself odd. She was about to explain, but caught herself. "I guess I never told your mother about it, so no way *you'd* know. Hey! Let's unload your car and get you settled before we talk about boring life stuff." Trinity briskly scooted by me and out to my car for the first trip without even putting on her shoes. Already this lady was proving to be *quite* the character.

Over the next hour, I was blessed with an immense amount of help from Trinity unpacking my car and carrying my things into the house. It didn't take me long to feel utterly wiped from the summer heat. Trinity was the opposite — she was like a freaking freight train! For each trip I made, she'd make three, typically carrying twice the amount. To some degree, I was a little humiliated how this 40-something lady was putting my personal fitness to shame.

It also didn't help that my room was on the second floor, meaning each trip demanded its own exhausting trudge up the thin, steep staircase. My room was like any other guest room you'd find. A simple bed, a simple table and dresser, and of course being Trinity's home, accented with nature decor. Not wanting to disrupt the flow, I opted not to unpack my personal items... at least right away.

As I sat on the bed to take in the ambiance, I heard Trinity climb the stairs with what should be my final bag. She tossed it on the ground triumphantly. "Aaaand... that's a wrap!"

My heart was still beating from the effort. "Seriously, *thank* you, Trinity. I'm floored by your stamina." I really meant it. This woman seemed like a total rockstar. Beautiful, in-shape, a homeowner... Everything about her was extremely impressive.

She humbly shrugged. "Hey, it takes a lot of energy to keep this place in tip-top shape."

Clearly incapable of rest, Trinity treated me to a full tour of the other rooms in her house. It was an aesthetically cohesive 2-bed, 2-bath home that, while low in square footage, certainly makes the most of its space. Each design choice was intentional and on-theme. Plus, for whatever space the inside lacked, the outside *more* than made up for it.

I must've been so zoned in on my car-clearing that I didn't even *notice* the pool in the backyard. It wasn't huge, but had some space for wading and went as deep as six feet. The entire pool area was surrounded by lush, colorful flowers and trees. It felt like a secret rainbow sanctuary.

Trinity pointed to an area behind the pool with a small path. "There's another garden area with a gazebo and some chairs back there. It's a great place to read or just relax."

"Trinity... this is astounding," I said, overwhelmed. "I had no idea what to expect driving up here, but..."

"Not this?" She finished my thought. "A lot of people say that. But hey, I'm a flower fanatic and take a lot of pride in appearance and quality — for both myself and my property."

She led us back into the kitchen for a snack and drink to bide our time until dinner, all while doing our best to catch up on 20 years of lost time. For as hectic and high-energy as she is, Trinity was a great listener and wonderful to chat with. I almost felt guilty spending time going over *my* own life, knowing hers must be 100 times more interesting. But after explaining my nursing job dilemma, I remembered to bring up the very first question I had for her while peering through the window.

"So... the dancing. You said that's something you're filming?" I asked.

"Ah! You're so right, I haven't given you the spiel yet." Trinity had me get up and follow her to the cleared out living room where the makeshift 'dance studio' was.

"So..." she huffed, as if ready to drop some crazy revelation. "This is gonna sound kinda weird, but I've always wanted to be an entertainer."

Huh? That's it?

"Uh, that doesn't sound weird at all," I assured her. "Lots of us have dreams like that."

"Well..." she continued. "After finding success in the corporate world so young — and then leaving that life in *glorious* fashion — I decided to take up being... an influencer."

I shrugged. "An influencer? Like on TikTok?"

"TikTok, Instagram... a little bit of Facebook. Basically companies send me products — everything from makeup to hair products to clothing... and I try 'em out, review them, and sometimes do silly little dances with them. Then people buy shit based on whether or not I like it or not. I post under the handle @PrincessTrinity. It's silly... but it's become my brand so I'm sticking with it!"

"That's... really interesting," I muttered, not really sure how to respond. I mean, it's objectively surprising that a woman in her 40s — especially one of her means — is trying to be an influencer.

Trinity sighed again. "Look, I did the whole corporate thing for nearly 20 years and it fucking burnt me to a crisp. I needed something fun, something I could work toward. I thought, 'Hey, *I* like beauty products. *I* have opinions. Why not try this out?'"

"And how's it going?" I asked, though feared I came across insensitive.

"Pretty well, I think. I have around 30,000 followers on

TikTok, 50k on Instagram. Facebook skews a little older so I'm not as big there..."

My eyes lit up. "Wow! That's... genuinely incredible." Nowadays, 30,000 followers isn't exactly rare, but it's still impressive for a nonprofessional.

Trinity let out a *huge* sigh of relief. "Phew! I'm glad you dig it because... look, while I love your mom, she's *very* traditional. I'm sure she'd lose her mind if she found out I flaunted clothes and makeup online for brands. I guess I was a little afraid you'd judge me for it too."

I confidently shook my head. "Not at all," I assured her, chuckling. "I mean, I'm probably the furthest thing from your target audience... but I support you 100%."

Feeling much more confident knowing I accepted her quirky side hustle, Trinity encouraged me to sit around as she walked me through her 'studio'. Admittedly, the influencer world — particularly the *beauty* influencer world — was of no interest to me. I don't like attention, I don't like performing... Keeping to myself with a good book is my idea of fun. But from an academic perspective, I appreciated her little crash course.

"So you film yourself dancing, I assume you edit and voice-over later... When do you actually *use* the products?"

"Like this! Here, I've got one left," Trinity said, opening up a tiny box she pulled from a white gift bag. Out of the delicate white box, wrapped in plastic, was a tiny metallic item. I stepped closer to her iPhone, positioned on a tripod and surrounded by a ring light for even lighting.

The metallic item turned out to be a deep-red lipstick tube, evident as she untwisted it and held it close to the camera.

"Step back please," she directed me as she was ready to hit 'record' on her phone. I stood there still as she pulled the lipstick from the camera toward her face, shook her body a little bit, then playfully applied it to her lips, ending the whole sequence with a big smile.

"Okay, all good," Trinity said, letting me be at ease.

"No review?" I asked.

"That comes later, during the voiceovers. I told you, it's a whole process. An insert here... a wide shot there..."

"Well, what's your first impression?"

Trinity shrugged. "I dunno. I need to see in a bigger mirror." She took one step toward the mirror on the living room wall, but suddenly stopped, almost tripping over herself.

That was weird. "You okay?" I asked, concerned. But she turned around to me with a little smile.

"Have you ever worn makeup before, Anderson?" she asked plainly.

I gulped, dumbfounded by her insane question. "Uhh... *no*?"

She chuckled quietly. "Because why get only *one* opinion on this pretty new lipstick, when I can get two?"

2

I don't think Trinity realized how strange her question was. If she had, she wouldn't be looking at me so matter-of-fact. Was this supposed to be a joke?

"I... I don't wear lipstick," I told her with full sincerity, though my voice was wavering a tad.

"I know. You *said* that. I'm suggesting you try it on and give me your thoughts. Always better to have a second opinion."

A million reasons for why this was a dumb idea popped in my head. And still, I was blown away by Trinity's earnestness. My Aunt — a forty-something beauty product influencer — wanted to share her interest with me. So in that regard her proposal was actually kind of sweet. But 'sweet' doesn't mean 'rational'.

My face was stuck in this weird, uncomfortable contortion as I mulled over her question. My prolonged silence and hesitation was becoming funny to her.

"Oh, don't be such a little wuss," Trinity teased. "Life's all about trying new things! It's not like you'll be on camera."

Hmm... She's right. It's only the two of us after all. I stared across the room at Trinity, playfully twisting the tube of lipstick in her hand. The sound of the twisting tube was like a siren's song, luring me toward disaster.

"Okay but *you* have to put it on me," I said, finally backing down.

Trinity was ecstatic. "Yes! You'll look so darling, I guarantee it." She grabbed my hand and pulled me closer, molding her mouth into a weird shape. "Put your lips like this and try not to move."

I did as told, standing as still as possible while she gracefully applied the product to my lips. It didn't take long — 15 seconds at most — but her reaction suggested I looked like a whole new person. "Ah, I knew it! You *do* look darling."

Enough already. I had to see myself. I scooted around Trinity to a mirror hanging in the living room and...

Wow.

I didn't exactly look like a different person, but the bold red pop on my lips changed the entire energy of my face. It was as if my face had a secret femininity that was unlocked by the red lips. My bold, brown eyes, thin nose, and tight jawline suddenly seemed softer and girlier paired with the new lip color.

"That's the power of makeup," Trinity said, giggling as she watched me purse my lips in the mirror. "A good lip can change a face for the better."

"I don't know if I'd say 'for the better'..." I replied cynically. "I look like a freaking girl!"

Trinity came up behind me and tugged at my hair tie, loosening my brunette ponytail and letting it fall onto my shoulders. Her eyes widened. "Nope. Because *now* you look like a freaking girl!"

One look at myself with my hair down and the red lipstick and I nearly lost it. I retreated from the mirror, overwhelmed by this new, shockingly feminine appearance. "Okay, that's it! We're done here. This is too freaky."

Trinity was dying with laughter. "You're so sensitive! Are you always this jumpy?"

"No, but I'm also not normally wearing lipstick with my hair down!" I snagged a tissue from the table and started rubbing my lips to get the makeup off as fast as possible. Trinity rushed over to stop me.

"Wait, you promised me a review!" she pestered, grabbing the tissue from my hands. "Just tell me, what did you think?"

Seriously? Was furiously removing it not a clear enough answer? "*Freaky*. That's my review."

She rolled her eyes. "Ugh, you boys could really learn to lighten up. I actually thought you looked pretty."

"I know. I did. *That's* the problem," I told her firmly.

Trinity must've gotten the message by now because she held up her hands in defeat. "Alright, alright. You win. Thank you for trying, I guess."

I didn't like how things had gotten so tense so quickly after such a nice time unpacking my car and touring the house. Maybe I was just on edge after a long day of travel.

"I'm... I'm gonna hop in the shower and chill in my room for a bit," I told her, still a little uneasy. "Go ahead and finish your work for the day."

As I came to learn, Trinity was not the type to hold a grudge. She left me alone to unpack my things and set up what'd be my home for at least the next couple months. Neither the lipstick nor anything beauty-related was brought up the rest of the day. She must've realized her overstep and that pushing makeup on boys is not the best way to garner trust.

But that evening, she more than made up for it by preparing a lovely first dinner for the two of us — delicious tofu stir-fry. Trinity, like myself, was a vegetarian. But unlike myself, Trinity was an *excellent* cook. I always thought that the best cooks are able to fill you up twice: first with the smell, and later with the taste.

Already I could tell that living with Trinity would be safe, nurturing, and peaceful. In many respects that was ideal — after all, who *doesn't* want a secure home life? But I had to be careful not to get too comfortable. My time in Old Buffalo wasn't going to last forever, and I had my eye firmly on the next stage of life — a nursing job at a glitzy, downtown Chicago hospital.

These days, an ADN degree doesn't get you much, especially in the hyper-competitive Chicagoland area. In order to get a decent job, I'd either need a *Bachelor's* degree in Nursing (which I don't have), or a passing score on the NCLEX exam — which we call 'the boards'. Passing the boards would give me the RN designation necessary for a fighting chance. In fact, ADNs are already in an uphill battle against BSNs... but hey, it's the hand I've been dealt and the one I'm gonna play. So my 'job' for the next couple months is to study-up and make myself the best possible candidate... whatever that entails.

I communicated this clearly to Trinity, and she was supportive of my studies. I'd have my space, she'd have hers. We'd respectfully live our separate, very different lives.

"Morning! Sleep okay?" Trinity asked with pep as I trudged downstairs to the kitchen. Damn, I thought that getting up at eight in the morning I'd be the first one up, but it looked like she'd already returned from a run and was halfway into cooking breakfast.

"Fine, thanks," I said through a yawn. I peered over the pan. "Are those sausage links?"

"*Beyond* sausage," she replied. "I'm in love with that fake meat stuff. It's a vegetarian's mistress!" Trinity flipped the links another time and determined them ready. "Want some?"

I checked the time on my phone. "Sure, but I'm eating quick today. My plan is to treat studying like a 9 to 5 job. There's a library nearby right?"

"Good on you! And there sure is. It's in that sleepy part of downtown near city hall. Nice area to walk around too."

I snacked on my fake meat links and a couple eggs Trinity scrambled up as well. "Any plans for you today?"

"Gotta film a couple videos this morning. Then I'll probably swim some laps at the club. Oh! And I got some things I need to bring down from the garage attic..."

"Jeez, active day!" I replied.

Yesterday's dinner conversation all but confirmed that Trinity was in the 'upper class' of Old Buffalonians. Not only was she a homeowner, but she was a member of Golden Dunes Country Club. By the sound of it, anybody who's anybody was a member there. Old money, new money... as long as you *had* money and lived in Old Buffalo, you were a member of Golden Dunes.

As tempting as an invite to her glamorous club was, I politely declined for today with my sights set on studying. One tasty breakfast later and I was off to the library.

My second time driving through downtown Old Buffalo was much more thought-provoking. I wondered who lived where and who belonged to Trinity's club. What did these people think of out-of-towners like myself and the thousands of other Chicagoans who made Old Buffalo their summer home? Was it frustrating, or did they appreciate the economic boost? Still, for essentially a vacation town, Old Buffalo looked like any other in the midwest: quaint and quiet.

Exactly as Trinity said, the library was directly across the street from the impressive city hall building — but certainly not overshadowed. The twin buildings were architectural marvelous — twin gothic, limestone beasts looming over the town with matching, massive lawns out front. I wondered if that was intentional. Clearly the town took great pride in its public buildings — a quality I really appreciated, even if much of that enjoyment was given to people who only lived here three months of the year. But maybe I'm just wasting my time thinking about the locals knowing the goal of coming here is just to leave as fast as possible.

In the large main room of the library I found a giant wooden table to claim for the day. Though I tried my best to be quiet, I noisily spread out my study materials around the giant table: notecards, notepads, binders, my laptop, and several textbooks.

I've always been a chaotic studier. Heavy on practice materials and verbal repetition. You could argue that a public library is the *worst* place for this, but I also didn't want to bother or be bothered by Trinity's filming. A barren, mid-day library did just the trick as long as I could keep my voice down.

Outside of a 45-minute jaunt to a sandwich shop for lunch, I was pretty much trucking through the day uninterrupted. My only concern was the precipitous loss in retained nursing school information. Hell, I'd only graduated a couple weeks ago and I felt like there were so many facts and practices that weren't immediately coming to me. But still, I knew with diligent work and focus I could pull off being fully prepared by the end of August.

I was rolling, I was locked-in... That is, until my phone rang just before 4. Not a text, a *call*. It was Trinity. Ducking my head and hushing my voice, I answered.

"Hey, what's up? I'm in the library so I can't re—" I began but was quickly cut off.

"Is this Anderson Saffron?" a voice asked. A *man's* voice. It was Trinity's number but this *wasn't* Trinity.

I suddenly felt a little scared. "Uh... yes. Who is this?"

"Excellent. Just giving you a heads up that your Aunt is in the hospital. *Please* don't worry, she's gonna be fine. She just had a fall."

"A *fall!?*" I exclaimed, much to the annoyance of the other library-goers. "Sorry... uh..."

Thankfully, the man jumped in with an address for the hospital. I hung up the phone in shock. "A fall?" I whispered to myself as I hurriedly packed up my things and shuffled out of the library.

A KIND GREETER directed me to the first floor room where Aunt Trinity apparently was recovering. Blessings of a small town hospital I suppose — no hour-long corridors to traverse just to find a patient room.

The floor was pretty dead when I arrived. Nothing like the hospitals I was accustomed to with nurses and physicians buzzing around, busy as bees. In fact, I was actually halted not by a medical professional, but the admin assistant.

"Hey hey hey," she held up her hand, preventing me from going into the room. "Anderson?"

I skidded to a stop. "Yeah, what?" Ugh, that sounded harsh... "I'm sorry, I'm in a rush."

The woman in her 60s smiled sweetly. "I imagine so! Just so

you know, your Aunt *is* okay... but she might look a little... shocking."

"It's okay, I'm a nurse," I answered confidently.

"Oh, you are? Good! I'd ask where you work but I'm sure you're in a rush."

"Unemployed at the moment. Studying for boards," I answered a little dismissively and walked briskly into the room. I hate coming across as rude, but this wasn't exactly a time for chit-chat.

I lightly knocked on the door and opened it, just as I had when arriving at Lumber Lane. But instead of a bouncy, bright Aunt Trinity, she was in *far* worse condition.

Amidst the jungle of medical equipment, bedding, and bandages sat a person. "Trinity?" I asked, concerned.

"Mmhm!" I heard from the body. A little muffled, but surprisingly peppy. "Hey!"

Now, I should say as a nurse, I've seen blood, cuts, bruises... you name it. So Trinity's appearance didn't exactly *bother* me, but she certainly didn't look like her normal, gorgeous self either. There she sat, propped up in the bed with a bandage over about half of her face like a poorly-wrapped mummy. Her left arm was in a sling and had thick, bulky padding on her right shoulder. The other hand was resting on her lap in a splint while the rest of her body had a smattering of bandages covering up what must be scrapes, bruises, or even worse.

"How silly do *I* look, huh?" she muttered. I couldn't believe she could have a sense of humor at a time like this.

"What... what *happened?*" Was all I could manage.

She sighed and looked at me with her one visible eye. "Forgive me if I'm not too wordy because this all hurts like *hell*... but I was cleaning out the attic and had a terrible fall down the stairs. Caught myself... *kinda...*" she gestured to her shattered arms. "And it led to a full-on face plant."

"Oh... my... god..."

"Yep... Thankfully the garage door was open and my neighbor Andrew walked by at just the right moment. I felt like Kate Winslet at the end of Titanic, yelling for help with any breath I could muster. Except I didn't have a whistle and it wasn't freezing water."

So Andrew must've been the man that called me. "Jesus... What'd they diagnose you with?"

Well, I haven't seen an ortho doc yet, but my hand and shoulder are super fucked up. Must have a couple broken fingers too... *And* my nose. I mean, falling 12 feet onto solid concrete will do that!"

"I'm sure..." I said, still taking in the horror of her condition.

"They're keeping me here for a few more hours while things get figured out. Mind sticking around?"

I took a step toward my Aunt and tenderly placed my hand on the side of her bed. I was afraid if I touched her, I'd only break another one of her bones. "Of course of course of COURSE!" I said emphatically. "Anything you need, okay?"

Trinity sighed and gave me her best pain-free smile. "I'll have the doc explain more to you since you guys speak the same medical language." Another deep sigh from Trinity, followed by what seemed like a painful cough. "Fuck! Everything hurts."

"I know, I know..." I replied gently, still standing next to the bed. "Shitty start to the summer."

"The worst. And right after swimming my fastest quarter mile ever," Trinity lamented. "I'm sure you figured, but I'm gonna need a little help around the house for the next couple days."

I chuckled. "*Weeks*, probably. But sure. Whatever you need, I'm here for you. I'll mix in my studies with all the caretaking you need, okay?"

Another smile, but this one a little less sure. "That'd be great. But you know... There's also a *job* I can no longer do."

I raised an eyebrow at her, afraid of what she was about to ask. But Trinity was nothing if not earnest. "I know you're a boy and all — and I *know* you despised that lipstick. But maybe you can lend a hand reviewing a few more products? Princess Trinity could really use the help..."

3

I desperately wanted to help out Trinity. I mean, *look* at her! She's in seriously deep shit. But just because her arms aren't working, doesn't mean her brain isn't.

"Uh... let's talk about that later," I said, not wanting to outright reject her at the moment, but still wishing to convey sympathy. It was a punt, sure. But a necessary one. Right now, the thing she needed most was company and comfort. So that's exactly what I provided for the next couple hours, as we talked, laughed, and kept things light.

Not wanting to be stuck with an overnight hospital bill, Trinity opted to be taken home in the late evening. She'd had an exhausting day and needed rest more than anything. The results of her MRI would be coming tomorrow, but neither of us were counting on good news. What more could I do than get her safely in bed, help rewrap her wounds, and keep her as comfortable as possible.

"Mhmm..." Aunt Trinity murmured, listening to the doctor as he delivered the results over the phone. "I guess it's not too surprising... What about a timeline?"

Trinity and I were seated around the kitchen table, listening to the doctor's verdict on speaker phone from her cell.

"You're lucky it's not worse, honestly," he said frankly. "Your broken nose should heal up fine without treatment. A few weeks there. The left pinky finger will need to stay in that splint for maybe a month." The doctor paused, then delivered the major blow. "The hand and shoulder... Those will take a while. No surgery, thankfully. But a couple months, maybe, to get back to normal. And that's before even starting physical therapy."

"And all the facial brushing?" Trinity asked, strangely concerned about *that* element the most.

"Like I said, the nose'll heal on its own. The swelling and scratches will too. These things just take time, Trinity. Just hold off on headshots or yearbook photos for a while."

I chuckled, but Trinity sighed. "I understand. Thank you."

We signed off with the doctor and Trinity, for the first time, slumped in her seat. The ever-positive woman was finally beat down.

"You know, it *could* be way worse," I said, parroting the doctor's words.

"Yeah, it could..." she admitted. "There's just so much I wanted to accomplish around here this summer. I was thinking about re-doing a bunch of landscaping, I had my swimming goals..."

"Well, I could always drag you behind me in the lap pool," I kidded. Trinity laughed again, somewhat painfully as she clutched her shoulder.

God, did I ever feel bad for her. I could tell this physically broken woman was fighting to keep her spirit intact. A splint on her finger, a brace on her hand, and that shoulder sling made her look like an injured war vet. Not to mention her face, which hadn't improved much since yesterday. Her lips, eyebrows, and forehead were all cut, scraped, and covered by bandages. Half of her face was a sickly, purple-yellow from the bruising.

"How about this... The mornings will be for me to study. Then when the afternoon hits, I'll run your errands, do your yard work, and complete any chores you need."

Trinity's face lit up. "Seriously? That'd be lovely!" she exclaimed. "Ah! I honestly can't thank you enough. I promise, I'll think of a way to repay you."

As much as I wanted to ask for money, my heart deep down couldn't accept payment for this kind of work. She was giving me free room and board, after all. If there's one thing my parents instilled in me, it's that you help out your family — no questions asked. And even so, it's not the *worst* idea to practice my caretaking and nursing skills.

FOR THE NEXT SEVERAL DAYS, my schedule went exactly as planned. I'd wake up and help Trinity with whatever she needed physically — dressing, bandage changing, medications... With such limited mobility of her hands and upper body, even simple tasks were a massive struggle if unassisted. So I realized a helpful daily task would be prepping for her breakfast and lunch in the mornings.

From morning to lunchtime, I'd camp at my now go-to table at the library, studying away and desperately clinging to anything I'd retained from two years of nursing school. Even if I hadn't learned much in the short time, I'd at least gotten better at *quietly* shuffling my books, binders, and papers to avoid mean glares.

I'd return to Trinity's in the early afternoon for a quick lunch, then jump straight into her to-do list. Each day brought its own unique challenge or task, though thankfully I had Trinity right there to teach or explain how to do things. I was a little ashamed how *not* handy I was. I mean, jeez, I didn't *think* I was so sheltered growing up, but my lack of familiarity with gardening tools and lawn care trinkets was exposing all my weak points.

A great example was when the freezer door handle was busted and needed to be re-screwed.

"There's an allen wrench in the garage—" Trinity began, to which I replied with a blank stare. "*Really?*" she added. "God, your Dad taught you *all* the wrong things…"

Funny enough, I felt like I was making more progress as a homeowner/landscaper/errand boy than I was being an actual nurse.

The best part about this rhythm though was, at the end of the day, Trinity and I would spend an hour or so in the kitchen making a delicious dinner for the two of us. With her brain and my hands, we cooked up some pretty tasty vegetarian dishes. Only one week in and I was growing more and more comfortable with her. Hell, I lived with my *own* mom for my entire life — and of course, I love her to death — but I never really developed an adult relationship with her. Aunt Trinity was different. Closer to me in age, similar-ish stages in life... She felt like the mix of a mother and older sibling mixed into one.

By my second week we'd already set the precedent that Wednesdays would be movie nights. A week ago, she was in much worse shape and barely cared what I threw on. This week, she put her foot down as tonight's decider. I guess I'd call it progress.

"You ever seen 'She's All That'? Because if you haven't, it's essential."

I shook my head. "No, but even the title sounds like a shitty rom-com."

"It's *absolutely* a shitty rom-com. And *that's* why you need to see it," Trinity insisted, motioning for me to pick up the remote and queue it up. She didn't have cable, but I found it after digging through a couple streaming services.

I'd never heard of this movie before, but it didn't take long to realize it was basically that old musical, 'My Fair Lady'. Essentially, Freddie Prinze Jr. bets his friend that he can transform the nerdy Rachel Leigh Cook into the next prom queen. And *shocker*, he starts to fall for her.

The movie was charming and goofy enough to warrant a watch, and if anything, I enjoyed Trinity quoting certain lines and reminiscing about the first time she watched it. Trinity is *definitely* a movie talker, too — something I normally wouldn't have the patience for. But hey, tonight's her night.

As the movie hits its third act, there's a scene where Rachel Leigh Cook waltzes downstairs, beautifully transformed into a prom queen. It's a sweet moment, they play that 'Kiss Me' song in the background... It's great. I looked over across the living room at Trinity, wondering if she was a movie *crier* in addition to a talker, but she wasn't crying. In fact, through the bruised coloring on her face, I noticed an idea formulating.

"Can you pause the movie?" she asked. I did as told and she looked over at me.

"You never told me if you'd help me out with the beauty products," she said bluntly. Notably, it wasn't a question. She worded it almost as an accusation — though not that aggressive.

I admit, her question didn't completely catch me off guard. After all, this movie's all about transformation and letting beauty products turn you into something you're not.

"No, I haven't," I answered honestly. "I kinda thought you just didn't care."

Trinity softened her tone. "I don't want to seem unappreciative, but... I dunno, this movie's making me feel like I'm missing out. I have such good momentum with the influencer thing, and I got a backlog of all these products I wanna review. But... *look* at me."

Her face looked better than it did a week ago, but a shoulder sling, a brace, a splint, and bruises galore don't exactly lend themselves to the beauty influencer look.

"So what're you suggesting? You wanna doll me up like a prom queen and have me waltz down the stairs?" I asked, completely joking, but quickly afraid I planted a seed in her head.

"No, no... just, like I said, lend a hand in that department. I need content for my pages. I'll do all the posting and captioning. I just... I need a temporary model."

I thought about her request for a moment. She must've caught me in the exact right mood, because her words didn't sound *so* absurd this time around. "Alright... What do you have in mind?"

"Well, I got this super cute nail polish that I've been meaning to show off. Obviously, nobody wants to look at a splint or a brace so–"

"Sure," I answered confidently. "Nail polish I can do."

She raised an eyebrow. "*Seriously*? Wow, I honestly thought you—"

I didn't have much patience for dissecting my acceptance of wearing nail polish. "I guess you just caught me in a good mood."

If it weren't for her injuries, she would've jumped for joy and applauded. But Trinity looked as happy as can be. "Ooh! Can I paint your nails during the movie? There's just enough time left that it'll work out. I can use my left hand, too!"

"Uh..." I muttered, not expecting this to start so quickly. "I guess..."

Trinity had me fetch the bottle of nail polish that was boxed up in the closet near the front door with the rest of her unopened, gifted products. I grabbed the small black box she told me about, perched right on top of the looming mountain of unboxed girly products. I shut the door and returned to the dimly lit, quiet living room.

"Sit here, let me show you," Trinity said calmly, as I took my seat next to her on the couch. I gulped, more than a little nervous as I removed the bottle from its packaging. It was a bright, baby blue color. I hadn't been this nervous around my aunt since the lipstick moment on my first day here. The vision of myself in the mirror, looking almost entirely like a girl from only *lipstick*. Would nail polish create the same stomach-churning feeling of a feminine Anderson?

But just as I screwed the top off the bottle to begin, Trinity shifted away. "Phew!" she said, scrunching her face. "You, uh... Did you shower after yard work today?"

"I... Uh... I guess I didn't," I said mindlessly, still focused on the impending nail polish. "Sorry, we went right into cooking—"

"Oh, it's no problem," she assured me, giggling. "But can you blame me if I wanna avoid smelling your stink for the next half-hour?"

I turned bright red with embarrassment. Here I was about to get my nails done by my Aunt, and *now* she was telling me I stink. But I took the awkwardness as an escape route. "Fine, I'll go shower. So nails tomorrow?"

Trinity shook her head. "No, still nails tonight. We have a movie to finish!"

I shrugged, accepting her request. But I took only one step upstairs before she called my name again.

"Anderson? I actually have a better idea. Can you use *my* shower?" she asked politely.

I stared at her, confused. "...why?"

"I want to paint *all* of your nails and take pictures for the page. Toenails too. So that means I'll need freshly shaved legs for the pictures."

4

What started as a movie night was rapidly turning into much more. First, an innocent little 90s movie. Then a nail request. *Then* a mandated shower followed by a request to shave my legs??

As much as I thought Trinity's request was absurd, I more so didn't want to ruin what was a peaceful, relaxing evening. If shaving my legs for a couple of pictures would make her happy, then that's exactly what I'll do.

"Yeah, that's fine..." I huffed, hiding my resistance. "I don't really know *how*... but, like, I can try."

"Well, obviously I'm not gonna be much physical help," Trinity said, wiggling her brace. "Nor do I want to get *that* personal with ya! But I have a few razors and some shaving cream in the bathroom. I'll talk you through it through the door."

In for a penny, in for a pound, I suppose.

I fetched a change of clothes from my room upstairs and brought it back down to Trinity's master bathroom. Other than a peek into her bedroom during the initial tour, I had no reason to be in here. Yet here I was, disrobing in my aunt's master bathroom, waiting for the shower to heat up so I could transform into her hairless leg model.

I should note that I'm *already* nearly hairless. My mother is a blonde Irishwoman with extremely fair skin and my father is half-Chinese — both of which contribute to minimal, light hair on my legs, face, and underarms. I remember teammates on the JV tennis team in high school making jokes about me. But here I was for the first time in my life, seeing it as a surprising benefit.

"Little body hair is *still* body hair," Trinity clarified, sensing I may be trying to get out of shaving at the last moment. "Trust me, it'll be simple."

Naked and uneasy, I stepped into the warm, soothing stream and let the water wet my skin. It was an extremely nice shower. The intricate, funky tile design on the sides that served as a nice distraction to my discomfort.

"Wash up first. It'll exfoliate the skin and make the razor glide easier," she shouted through the door. I foolishly didn't bring my own shampoo or body wash, so rather than dry off and get it myself, I opted to use Trinity's. But it may have been a mistake, because her selection of soap couldn't have been girlier.

"Lavender Bliss?" I read the body wash aloud to myself, but Trinity must've heard.

"Oh please, it won't bite! Plus it's got little scrubby things in it to clear out dead skin. I got it as a brand gift!"

Jeez… I wonder what *that* TikTok video would've been like. Not looking to put up a fight, I washed my whole body til I was clean and lavender-scented. "Okay, done!"

"Are you due for a hair wash?" she asked.

"Uh, yeah, but…"

"Just try out mine. It smells super pretty."

Again, I didn't *want* to smell pretty. I didn't *want* to be doing any of this. But sure enough, I threw her a bone and washed my long, brunette hair with her 'Strawberry Fields' shampoo and conditioner.

I'd been in the shower for a while, so I figured I must be appropriately soaked and exfoliated.

"Can I *please* shave now?" I complained.

"Yes you may," Trinity answered. She talked me through the shaving gel application process and explained how smooth, consistent strokes were best for getting rid of hair. I was a little embarrassed how little came off, but after around three minutes of concentrated effort and a thorough rinse, my legs were smooth and clean as a whistle.

"Alright, done and done," I said satisfied, shutting off the water and snagging my towel. I changed into my fresh t-shirt and pair of shorts before unveiling my newly smooth legs to my aunt.

Trinity studied my legs almost academically, getting low for the closest possible look. "Hmm, good work! And not even a nick. You're sure this was your first time?"

"Yes!" I spat out, immediately blushing. I felt embarrassed even though I was telling the truth.

She gave her best one-shoulder shrug. "Then I guess you're a natural."

Of course, shaving my legs was only the prelude to Trinity's real request of painting my finger *and* toenails. I took my seat back on the couch next to her as we uncapped the bottle of polish and she began talking me through the painting process once again.

"This'll be a super simple post. No video, no dancing, just a picture of your pretty new hands and feet."

I was grateful that my favor to her didn't involve leaping around like a monkey... but the thought of having 20 baby blue nails wasn't exactly ideal either. With only her pinky and ring fingers in the splint, Trinity was able to adequately paint my first fingernail with reasonable precision and extend a proper tutorial.

"We'll do one coat, let them dry, followed by another coat," Trinity narrated as she started my second one. "I love that you keep them so long."

"They're not *that* long," I fought back, though realizing on a closer inspection it *had* been a while since I cut them.

"Well, you keep 'em neat, which I appreciate." Trinity handed me the brush. "You try."

It took me a few attempts to get it right, and we had a tissue at the ready to correct any mistakes before drying. But once I was finally on a roll, we unpaused the movie and hung out as I gradually applied the baby blue polish to my nails. Every minute or so, Trinity would glance down to admire my work with a little head nod. Whether or not I liked painting my nails, it was nice to know I was at least *good* at it.

Painting my toes was pretty much the same deal, but this time I could use my dominant hand for each. Everything but the pinky toes were pretty much a breeze. Those required a bit more focus and precision.

"Lovely, lovely work," Trinity complimented as I was nearly finished. "Look at you, all pretty with your blue nails!"

I blushed, turning red like the lipstick from yesterday. "Hey, I'm just a nephew helping his aunt."

"Can you do mine?" she requested, wiggling her toes in front of me. "We can match!"

Only for a second did I think it was a *little* weird to touch my aunt's feet, but I decided to oblige anyway. Isn't that a thing girls do at sleepovers? Paint each others' nails? Why should this be any different? Not that *this* was a girls' sleepover... but the point stands.

If anything, this was just extra practice for my dexterity and nail-painting skill. Trinity held her feet perfectly still while I delicately applied the matching baby blue to her toenails. Funny enough, not only did our toes now match, but I also clocked her 'lavender bliss' scent. She smelled extraordinarily feminine and I couldn't help but wonder if I smelled equally as girly.

Her nails were painted to satisfaction and I returned to my chair for the remainder of the movie. It concluded predictably, with — spoiler alert — the two main characters falling for each other. Shocker again! I always found it funny how some women get so choked up over these predictable plots. Whether it had to do with her injuries or not, Trinity cried as the credits rolled.

"God, what's gotten into me?" She sniffled, stopping her

tears abruptly. "That movie's just so sweet. Did you like the ending?"

I rolled my eyes. "Well, I was busy focusing on *your* nails, so..."

She chuckled, admiring my work for probably the 50th time. "Heh, well, I'd say it's worth it."

Trinity rose from the couch as I cleaned up the snacks and drinks we consumed during the movie. The vibe of the night felt normal, aside from the fact I now had freshly shaven legs and pretty blue nails. The house was peaceful and serene with soft lighting conducive to slumber. Outside was dark and quiet, with only minimal noise coming from cicadas chirping in trees. I assumed that painting my nails would only cause disruption and chaos but clearly, the opposite was true. Trinity and I actually had a pleasant evening together.

"I think I'm off to bed," she announced with a big yawn.

I looked at her pointedly, expecting another feminine request. "No pictures tonight?"

She shook her head. "Eh, I'm too sleepy. I've got some ideas for tomorrow. Just don't grow too much leg hair overnight, 'kay?"

I laughed and said goodnight, though wishing she would elaborate on those ideas. I guess like everything else around here, I'll just hang tight for another surprise.

I WOULD NEVER HAVE GUESSED it, but the sensation of hairless legs on quality sheets? Simply unmatched. Hell, regardless of

Trinity's plans for the pictures, I might just have to keep my legs shaved purely for comfort. The world's ladies are certainly on to something.

It was unclear what Trinity had in mind for today, but upon exiting my room at the top of the stairs I was a little bit spooked. I heard a voice downstairs talking to Trinity. Who the hell did she have over? If it was a friend, it'd be the first I'd seen since moving in.

Sure enough, there were two ladies lounging in the living room, chatting away. Trinity, of course, and an unknown brunette woman with a bob cut, probably 10 or so years older than Trinity. I nearly whipped around the corner to go introduce myself but stopped suddenly, remembering what my hands and feet looked like.

Trinity must've heard me though. "Anderson, you there? Come meet my friend Tara."

"I... Uh..." I stood there motionless, obscured behind the wall. Trinity must've picked up on my hesitancy.

"Oh, heh. Your *nails*. Tara knows and she doesn't care. In fact, come show her how we match!"

I reluctantly slinked into the living room, giving Tara a friendly nod and trying desperately to hide my embarrassment.

Beyond her extremely sunburnt skin, Tara looked like the typical mid-50s midwestern woman. Short hair, a little on the heavy side... she reminded me a bit of my own mother. Her eyes darted directly to my nails.

"*Beautiful!*" Tara exclaimed. "You did this yourself?"

I hated that *this* was what we were discussing. "Well... Trinity showed me how."

"It's a really beautiful shade," she said, turning to Trinity. "This'll be in a video?"

"That's the plan," Trinity said.

"Uh, you said *pictures*," I quickly reminded her of our promise last night.

"Ah, yes. Pictures. My mistake," she apologized. "We'll take some beautiful pictures for a post."

Tara took one last sip of her coffee and stood up. "I should get out of your hair. It's so nice to know you feel better. And Anderson, *lovely* to meet you. I'm extremely impressed by your willingness to care for your aunt on top of your studies."

So she *did* tell her more about me beyond my nail polish. That's good. Tara was about to leave but Trinity looked like she had more to say.

"Tara, wasn't there something else?"

"Oh, yes! Trinity was telling me you used to play tennis in high school? You know, we're always looking for help in the summer at the Golden Dunes courts. One of the local kids just dropped out for the summer and we could use someone to take some shifts at the desk."

Another job? Jeez, I was really getting piled on here. Between studying, yard *and* house work, and caring for Trinity, that felt like a lot. "I... I'll think about it. Thanks."

"It's super low key," she assured. "Plus you can just study when it's quiet. But yes, think it over!"

Trinity walked Tara to the door and said goodbye. She gave me a little smirk. "You know, I didn't even *ask* about the job. She brought it up herself."

"Yeah, maybe."

"It's good for studying, you could earn some money — since you won't accept any from *me*," Trinity reminded me, though I rolled my eyes. We've had this talk before.

"Maybe, alright? Like I said, I'll think it over," I asserted, looking to change the subject. "Hey, speaking of work, what's the schedule for today? Am I doing pictures before or after studying?"

"How about right now?" Trinity suggested. "Just a few pictures, as promised."

I was ready to get this over with. We'd take the pictures, I'd remove the polish from my hands and toes, and I'd head off to the library. Not that it'd be the *worst* thing to wear polish in front of random library-goers, but still. I looked around the room for a possible picture angle, holding up my hands at different angles and testing with my own phone.

"I'm gonna run to the bathroom before we get started." Trinity headed down the hall to her bedroom. "Got some accessories for you, just to enhance the pictures. In the kitchen!"

What? I don't remember accessories being part of the deal... But then again, if it's just hands and feet, I understand how it'd look better with a bracelet or a pair of flip flops.

"Uhh, sure..." I muttered as she disappeared into the master bathroom. Eager to get this over with, I walked into the kitchen to search for her accessories. But as it turned out, Trinity's 'accessory' request was a bit of an overstatement. Maybe even an outright lie. Why? Because in the center of the kitchen table wasn't a bracelet, an anklet, or a pair of shoes.

No no no... Laid out neatly for me was a pair of itty bitty, teeny tiny, women's denim *booty* shorts.

5

I simply couldn't believe my eyes. Trinity took a chance convincing me to shave my legs — a request which at least made *some* sense — but this? Why on *Earth* would she expect me to wear freakin' booty shorts just to take pictures of my hands and feet? It simply didn't add up.

My first thought was to storm into Trinity's room and tell her how much of an overstep this was. Even if my face wasn't going to be included in the pictures, that didn't give her carte blanche to put me in whatever little outfit she desired. In protest, I decided instead to plant my butt at the kitchen table and wait for her to explain herself. A few minutes passed as I did exactly that, waiting to pounce.

"Uh, *EXCUSE* me?" I said the moment she came out from the hallway. I tossed the shorts at her in a fit of frustration. "What the hell are you trying to talk me into?"

Trinity looked genuinely confused. "What?" she said as the

tiny shorts fell to the ground in front of her. "Those shorts aren't for you, Anderson."

I stared at her blankly. "They... Huh?"

"Yeah, they're for *me*. Tara brought 'em over because she thought they'd look cute on me. I guess they don't fit her daughter anymore." Trinity explained honestly, but a smile crept on her face. "You didn't actually think those were for you, did you?"

Now I was turning red. "Um, well, *yeah*. You said 'accessories'..."

At this point she was full on cackling. "Anderson, shorts aren't accessories. They're shorts!" She took a few steps into the kitchen and picked up some loose items. "*These* are accessories."

Trinity held up a jangly bracelet and two silver rings. Literally my first thought. *Shit...*

"I'm... I'm so sorry. I shouldn't have come out so hard."

She rolled her eyes. "You're fine, you're fine... Just put these on and we'll take some nice pictures."

Not looking to cause any more trouble, I thanked her for the jewelry and swiftly put it on. Instead of limiting ourselves indoors, Trinity opted to use her lush, flowery backyard as the backdrop. She couldn't exactly hold the camera at the desired angles with her busted hand, so I took my own hand and foot 'selfies' at her direction.

There was a lot more thought that went into these pictures than I expected. The angle of the sun, whether or not to use portrait mode, making sure colors in the background didn't distract from the product itself... Each choice had creative integrity to it that I was beginning to appreciate.

"You're quite good at this," I told her, still feeling bad about my lash-out.

Trinity smiled. "You don't get tens of thousands of followers if you suck." Give me the camera, I wanna do a pool shot.

I was instructed to sit next to the pool — yes, the pool I had used zero times since I arrived but spent ample time nearby, watering its surrounding foliage and cleaning the deck and storage shack. She suggested an interesting pose where I put one foot in the pool and the other kicked up high in the air. Barely anything below my knees was shown, so my men's shorts weren't an issue.

"Cute!" she exclaimed, struggling to get up from her crouched position. "I think we're done. These'll do great."

She quickly swiped through the photos taken on the phone, making quiet, verbal notes on which stood out to her and which didn't.

"Are you saying not *all* of my photos are Princess Trinity quality?" I joked.

"No, they are, they are..." she said. "It's just got me wondering — Everyone's gonna know this isn't me. Or at least they'll know it's not *Princess Trinity*."

Trinity had a good point. Many of the dances, videos, and pictures she *normally* took are near-impossible due to her injury. While I'm sure her audience (and the brands) would understand that she needs time to recover, Trinity can't have it both ways. Either she loses momentum, or she puts out an inferior product.

But then it hit me. "You know, it can still be the Princess Trinity 'brand', right? Who says each post has to be Trinity herself?"

She looked at me, a mix of surprise and thrill that I even *had* a take on the issue. "So we just... *tell* everyone this isn't me?"

"No sense lying to them. I could just be, uh, your substitute?"

"A substitute..." she repeated in a whisper. "That'd be *way* easier, not always having to resort to such tight shots."

We were really on to something. Trinity and I tossed ideas back and forth in a frenzy as we threw together what felt like an entirely new business plan.

"Princess Trinity's out, so her substitute steps in," she began.

"And if the brand keeps growing, you can even make a *new* channel... 'Trinity Does Shoes' or 'Trinity does Nail Polish'.... or whatever," I added.

"Yes! Yes!!" she lit up like a bundle of joy. "God you're brilliant, Anderson. I knew it'd be awesome having you here."

Trinity led the way back inside after our successful brainstorming session, both of us full of the warm fuzzies. Who could've guessed that Anderson Saffron, the *least* creative person on the planet, would actually be a help in this department.

Maybe we were a little ahead of our skis on the 'multiple spinoff businesses' concept, but the energy was there. Trinity felt jazzed and motivated to post for the first time since her injury. With our pictures done, I was ready to leave the editing, copywriting, and posting to her while I went off to the library. But she needed me for *one* more thing before heading out.

"Anderson, if you're gonna be my substitute, you'll need a character within the 'Princess Trinity Universe'. Got a girl name?"

A girl name. I mean... shit. That hadn't even crossed my mind. Even if I were to be anonymous, I'd still need a name. 'Substitute' doesn't have any zing to it.

"I'll... I'll let you choose it," I told her after some consideration. "You're the creative genius anyway."

"How about 'Andie'?" Trinity threw out. "But with an 'I-E' to make it a bit girlier? I think that'll be believable."

I shrugged. "Whatever you wanna call my character is fine by me." As good as it felt to help Trinity, I had to live my own life too. And that life was studying for boards.

"Ah-ah-ah..." Trinity added, just as I turned around. She wiggled her three available fingers, reminding me that I was still sporting blue nails.

I blushed. "Heh... Good catch. Got any remover?"

DESPITE ITS IMPORTANCE TO TRINITY, I still hadn't checked out *any* of the Princess Trinity social media pages. To be fair, I'm rarely on TikTok and Instagram, and my Facebook has been deactivated for God knows how long. Nor did I have a real *reason* to, or even an urge. After all, none of the content is tailored toward me, so why bother?

But things changed with my upcoming involvement, and I felt like a traitor *not* checking it out. Plus, the curiosity of being at the library for a few hours, wondering if the post with my feet and nails in it had gone live yet, was too much to bear. So I set aside my study materials for the moment, popped in my earbuds, and did what I probably should have a long time ago.

Trinity was absolutely right — she *was* a growing star. The tens of thousands of followers on TikTok were legit, and *damn* did she have quite the catalog. Dozens and dozens and dozens of videos were posted, each reviewing a seemingly different product. Some were dances, hopping on the latest trending sound. Others were simple, scrolling product shots with voiceovers narrating her opinions. Everything had clean, engaging captions alongside clear voice recording and beautiful... shall I say, cinematography? Trinity was a pro. Full stop.

For a woman fed up with the corporate world and looking to start anew, I'd call what she did an unabashed success.

Mere moments away from returning to studying, however, I refreshed the page and finally saw it: A new post featuring my legs sticking out into the pool.

I gasped quietly to myself and feverishly scanned the room to make sure nobody was watching — as if they'd even *care*. True to her word, the post introduced me as her substitute.

'Apologies for my absence, as I've been dealing with some injuries that prevent me from reviewing these lovely products. So in my place for just a little while will be my lovely niece, Andie. This is her introducing the adorable new polish from...'

The post went on to describe the product, plug the brand, and include the appropriate hashtags. At least on Instagram, it was the photo I took of myself with my legs from a seated position, stretched out and hanging over the pool. The second of the two-photo post was a simple close-up of my fingernails. As promised, it was nothing too revealing. Simple, elegant, and introductory.

I closed the app and resumed my studying, satisfied with her image decisions. While it definitely felt weird presenting as a girl, the post had a healthy amount of anonymity to it. I wasn't tagged, I wasn't *actually* named... After all, this was in pursuit of helping my aunt in trying times. If that meant being her niece for a little while, so be it. I'm down for the ride.

A FEW MORE HOURS OF diligent studying and I was back home that afternoon to take Trinity in for an eye appointment, pick up some groceries, and clean up a few things around the house before prepping dinner. On the menu for tonight was a pasta dish with green beans and almond gremolata — a supposed favorite of Trinity's and one she'd been wanting me to attempt since I got here. I was still by no means a master chef, but I was leaps and bounds better than the day I arrived.

As I stood there silently cooking, watching Trinity browse her phone, I couldn't help but wonder how the first Andie post was performing — at least compared to her others. Was it a massive success, or did the engagement drop precipitously upon realizing the upcoming posts *wouldn't* be of her?

I felt caught in a strange, dissonant pickle. On one hand, I kind of wanted these posts to fail because, to me, failure meant that *of course* I couldn't just shave my legs and apply some polish to pass as a girl. That'd be absurd, and anyone who falls for it is a sucker.

But that's only part of me. The other – perhaps more *significant* – side of me could... I dunno... use the win? My entire life I've been aggressively average. Did I make varsity on the tennis team? Nope, just JV. Did I go to college? Well, just an *associate's* degree. Have I become an *employed* nurse? Still working on that...

The fact is, for as strange as the circumstances are, I could use a win right here. It'd be nice to know that someone appreciated *something* about me, even if it's just for having skinny legs and cute fingers and toes.

"Tara texted me," Trinity said, breaking the silence.

"Oh yeah?" I replied, mid-testing a piece of pasta from the pot. "Did she ask if you liked the shorts?"

"Ha! No, she actually asked about you again. I guess they could really use a sub at the tennis club."

"Damn, that's — one, two... — twice in a *day*?" I counted jokingly. "Is she that desperate?"

"Did you think about it at all? You said you would."

I placed the wooden spoon down on the counter and faced my aunt. "Look, I can't just leave you vulnerable to the elements. You and the nursing exam are my two priorities. I can always make money later on."

She smiled. "That's very sweet of you. Really. But I did some thinking today. I've been feeling so much more agile and motivated since this morning — plus, my body's feeling way better. Definitely not *yardwork* better, but enough to take care of the simple things around the house." Trinity had an earnest look to her. "I mean it. I think I'll be fine if you take a couple shifts per week."

I knew that if Trinity got injured again while under my watch, I'd never forgive myself. But she seemed serious. A couple weeks may not be enough time to heal up fully, but it's enough to learn your limitations and make adjustments.

"Plus, she reminded me that you're welcome to bring books and study whenever it's not busy!"

Everything sounded reasonable. "You're *sure*?" I ask, giving her one last chance to back out.

"A thousand percent," she answered confidently. "Hey, it's your summer too!"

It's settled then. I'd give Tara a call in the morning to talk about details.

While Trinity was ecstatic, I was stuck with a simmering fear the rest of the evening that I might've just put too much on my plate. Caretaking, studying, and errand-work already felt like a full time gig. Now I was adding a whole new part-time job? Maybe I just had to remind myself that adulthood isn't *supposed* to be easy. If I can't cut it here, how am I ever gonna cut it as a full-time nurse?

I SPENT the rest of the evening alone in my room, reading my book. I figured with the addition of yet another job, alone time will become only more of a commodity.

I heard a knock on my door. "Got a sec?" Trinity said through the door.

"Yep," I said, getting out of my bed to open the handle for her. But she beat me to it.

"See? I *can* do some things on my own..." she joked with a sly smile.

I smiled. "Touché."

"I'm off to bed, but I realized we never went over the results of your debut today..." Trinity pulled out her phone.

"TikTok? Facebook? Instagram?" I prodded, more curious than I'd like to admit.

"Take your pick. They all did *great*."

Letting it sink in, a satisfied grin emerged on my face. "Wow, that's..."

"Impressive, I know," Trinity playfully finished my sentence. "Great engagement, plenty of kind folks wishing me a speedy recovery... and a lot of nice things to say about you."

"*Really*?" I said, though not terribly surprised. My legs *do* look good after all. "Do you think they could tell I'm a boy?"

She scoffed. "*Definitely* not. In fact... that's what I wanted to talk to you about." Trinity took a deep breath — the same kind of deep breath I'd seen a few times before when she's about to ask me for a favor. "I think we can take this a little bit further."

My eyebrow raised suspiciously. "How so?"

"If you're down for it... I think we should get Andie into some outfits."

6

You know how when you're playing fetch with a dog and the dog is having the time of his life while *you* just stand there, apathetically tossing the ball? This is what hanging out with Trinity feels like. Sometimes it's more about her than about you.

I already told her I was more than happy to help out with the Princess Trinity account. She *knows* this. But the idea that I will just wear *any* outfit she hands me? Ridiculous.

"Didn't we already go over this? With the, uh... jean shorts?" I reminded her.

"Of course, of course. I'm not suggesting you wear anything you don't want to wear. I'm just saying that by limiting our shots to arms and legs... Well, we're just leaving a lot on the table."

She wasn't wrong. Take one look at her page and you'll notice she reviews all *kinds* of products. Most of those posts *aren't* static shots. Instead dances, videos, mini-vlogs... Her posts are full of color, motion, and activity.

"So what are you suggesting?" I asked cautiously.

"That we go forward on a case by case basis. Brands send me things all the time. All I ask is that you're *open* to the idea of showcasing certain clothing that you're comfortable with. Face hidden, of course."

Knowing my likeness would be concealed was comforting, even if that implied I'd be wearing girls clothes at the same time. I had every right to tell her no, but once again, Trinity had seamlessly reframed a crazy-sounding idea into a reasonable request.

"Alright, deal," I finally answered after a little thought. "Just don't be surprised if I only pick androgynous outfits."

Trinity cheered. "Everything you put on will be your decision and your decision alone. I promise! You're the best, Anderson."

And with that, Trinity shut the door and returned downstairs to her quarters. *My decision alone,* huh? I had a feeling that wouldn't *actually* be the case knowing how persuasive she can be. But still, it felt nice to know the sentiment was there.

ONE WOULD THINK the idea of wearing women's clothing on camera would keep me up at night. But in all honesty, Princess Trinity was the *last* thing on my mind. That's because the first thing on my morning agenda was to give Tara a call to accept the Golden Dunes tennis offer. And just as Trinity predicted, Tara was over the moon.

"Yes!!!" she shouted through the phone so violently I had to pull the phone away from my ear. "God, this is such good news. I know you'll be a perfect fit."

Beyond filling out starting paperwork for payroll and a few other forms, I wasn't set to begin until Monday. A blessing in disguise, really, since I had some projects around Trinity's property of which I'd been *badly* procrastinating.

One of my more annoying tasks these past couple weeks was reorganizing her messy garage. Being alone in there always felt a little eerie, knowing I was often standing mere feet from her brutal accident. Each time I ascended or descended the stairs into the garage attic I went fifty times slower than was probably necessary. The last thing we needed was for *two* peoples' summers ruined due to injury.

The stress of my stacking responsibilities was a bit worse than I originally thought. Thankfully, Trinity recognized that. While she didn't hold back on needed errands and caretaking tasks, she was clearly laying off the social media dressing requests. At least for now...

"You'll find your groove at Golden Dunes," Trinity assured me at dinner, the evening before my first shift Monday morning. "Tara's a sweetheart. I'm not too familiar with the tennis scene there, but I imagine it's chill."

I sipped my water, hiding any nerves. "I'm sure you're right."

"Once you get the hang of things and the shifts slow down, it'll feel like you're being paid to study."

I wanted to believe her. I had no reason not to. But something deep down made me believe the opposite. Could my first ever experience at a country club *really* be as drama-free as she says?

Monday morning marked an interesting milestone for me because it was the first time since arriving in Old Buffalo that I ventured further than a couple miles from Trinity's house. Everything in Southwest Michigan is and feels extremely local. So driving more than a dozen miles up the road to Golden Dunes felt like traveling to an entirely different dimension.

Turns out, Trinity's tree lined, wooded neighborhood was nothing like Golden Dunes. For starters, the club was nowhere near the lake. Perhaps the members thought 'why spend significant time at two lakeside properties when I can afford to mix it up?'. The Golden Dunes estate was more desert-like than anything else. Tasteful stones, sand, and gravel were used in place of grass, and much of the foliage and scenery would probably feel more at home in Arizona than here in Michigan. Maybe it's a water-conservation thing? Who knows.

The golden gates at the entrance were a little on the nose. Jeez, do they *really* need to be that blatant about their wealth? Whatever happened to subtlety...

I was greeted by a grinning man in a black, crisp suit and service cap. I took this man to be the security guard, and rolled down my window as I approached the gaudy guard stand.

"Welcome!" he said warmly. "Guest of a member?"

Funny how he immediately knew I *wasn't* a member —

maybe from failing to recognize my car, but more likely assuming no self-respecting Golden Dunes member would dare drive a Kia hatchback.

"Uh, well, I'm starting work here today," I told him. "I work for Tara."

Until now I didn't realize I had no idea what Tara's last name even was. But he didn't give me any trouble. "Anderson, then!" He replied at the ready. "No problem, we're expecting you." He pressed a button to lift the gate arm and I drove through, flashing the man a thank-you wave.

The last and only time I ever went to a country club was when I was a little kid — and that's only because Dad's boss hosted some bougie fundraiser. It was a long time ago, but whatever memories I still had were trumped by the esteem of Golden Dunes. The desert theme persisted through my drive up the road — cacti and other rough, prickly plants that looked like they shouldn't even be able to survive Michigan's climate lined the streets. After my uphill climb, I finally got my view of the main clubhouse.

The Golden Dunes clubhouse was easily the most impressive structure I've ever seen in person. It was as expansive as it was impressive, stretching far and wide with its gleaming white walls and shining, golden stucco roof. It looked more like a mansion than anything else — though I suppose that's what its members are accustomed to.

Fearful I'd accidentally impose on a member, I took one of the furthest away parking spots in the lot. There were a few equally shitty cars out this way too, making me wonder if this was the standard for employees. I took my books, water bottle, sunglasses case, and a packed lunch with me. The closer I got to the clubhouse, the more self-conscious I grew, afraid I looked too much like a poor packrat clutching my loose belongings.

Why couldn't Tara have given me any arrival instructions? Or hell, *Trinity*. I abhor arriving places unprepared. But my guardian angel must've been watching over me, because the first person I saw walking out the front doors of the clubhouse was none other than Tara.

I nearly dropped my things as I ecstatically waved, hoping to catch her eye before I lost her. But she saw me, and ran over to give me a hand.

"Not a fan of bags?" she joked, lightening the load a bit by grabbing my water bottle and a few books.

"I left in a hurry this morning," I admitted, though catching my mistake. "Not that I'm normally late or anything!" Tara gave a hearty laugh as she told me not to worry.

The inside was even gaudier and more impressive. The founder of this club *must* be from Arizona or New Mexico or something on account of the southwestern theming. They even went as far to include taxidermied snakes and rabbits in the lobby's desert-themed mini-scenes.

"This way," Tara said, interrupting my staring. I badly wanted to ask her what the initiation fee was. *Or the minimum net worth* to get in. But I held my tongue.

I didn't get too much of a tour, but we passed by some offices, a bar, a restaurant, and an empty ballroom that all fit the high-class, southwestern vibe. Outside, I caught glimpses of the pool, the golf course, and in the distance, tennis courts. For some reason, I had trouble picturing Trinity walking around here. Sure, she definitely had a fancy *side* to her, but she wasn't uppity by any means. Did she have close friends here who could tell me more?

"What exactly is your title, by the way?" I spat out. "Not trying to like, uh, *vet* you or anything." I added with a nervous laugh.

Tara chuckled, getting a good sense of my odd, awkward personality. "Recreational Director," she answered. "Basically anything that's a fun, community activity, it's run by me." Then she rolled her eyes. "Except golf, of course. They *always* gotta do their own thing."

Funny how even a club like this had its own version of annoying elitists. There's always a bigger fish, I suppose.

Tara swiped her card and led us through the gates, finally revealing what I'd been itching to lay my eyes on the moment I arrived. And boy, did these Golden Dunes courts not disappoint. Having played tennis at a public high school, we were often relegated to courts at the local park or our school's two 'courts' that were in such disrepair, we had to stop using them due to constant weird bounces and injuries to players. But here, I didn't spot a single blemish! The outdoor facility held four courts overlooked by an attendant stand. At the moment, only one of the four courts was being used.

"I present to you… your post!" she announced as she led me behind the counter of the homey stand.

I took a quick look around. "Nobody working today?"

"Just me. We're undermanned so… today, I'm the man," Tara explained.

At first glance, this seemed like a clean, comfortable

working environment. I was about to ask Tara a question when two women approached the stand. They looked tennis-ready.

Tara put on a big, fake smile as she greeted the women. "Good morning, ladies!"

"Hi," one of them answered, somewhat dismissively. Like everyone else I saw, she had a fairly uppity demeanor to her. "9:30 reservation on Court 2."

Tara glanced over at a reservation sheet hanging to her left, confirmed the ladies had the court, then nodded. "Of course. All signed in. Any rentals today?"

The other woman with comically large designer sunglasses didn't answer, instead holding up her full tennis bag as if to say 'uh, no you *idiot*. I have everything.'

"Very well," Tara replied coolly. "Enjoy your match."

The women walked off to their court as Tara rolled her eyes. "You'll meet some characters."

I cringed. "Jeez, I hope they're not *all* like this."

"No, no.... most aren't," she assured. "Well, *several* aren't."

With a down moment, Tara took the time to give me her best tutorial on working the desk. The long and short of it was booking reservation times, making sure the right folks were on the right courts, and handling any rentals. If I were the first shift, I'd open. If the last, I'd close. Otherwise, it seemed like a lot of downtime — which was *perfect* for studying. Though I obviously wanted to get comfortable with the job before pressing my luck.

"It's a good gig, really. It's okay to be firm with the rules, but if a member ever pushes you too hard, come find me and I'll deal with it."

I wanted to ask if there had been any issues in the past worth noting, but I held my tongue. "Got it."

Tara glanced around, running through her mental checklist to see if she missed anything. "Oh! I'm so dumb..."

She said, digging through a back chest for something. "You've probably noticed all the employees around here wear white. It's our uniform and *very* important to the brand. I'm sure you understand. Size?"

"Uh, small," I answered.

Tara pulled out shirts and shorts that were neatly folded. "I'm sure we have some in here..."

I watched Tara nearly empty the chest of its contents, but she seemed to only find larges and extra-larges.

"Shit... We might be out of smalls. You good with a large?"

I chuckled. "I guess the baggy look *is* in. As long as the members don't mind."

She pondered for a second, then a little half-grin grew on her face. "I'm sure your Aunt would get a kick out of this..."

"Out of what?" I asked.

Tara reached back into the chest, pulling out what looked like a perfectly usable small-sized uniform. But when she held it up against her body, I realized it was *far* from usable.

Why? It was a girls' polo and a short, white, pleated skirt.

7

"Oh, uh... the large will do," I quickly answered her original question, pretending I couldn't see the girl's uniform she was holding right in front of my face.

Tara was full-on cackling at my embarrassment. "Ha! No no no, you know *exactly* what I meant. But alright, alright, just a suggestion. I figured if you're willing to wear girly stuff on TikTok, you'd do it in person too."

There wasn't enough time in that moment to explain to Tara the intricacies of my deal with Trinity. I couldn't just say 'well actually, I'll be concealing my face... while also technically presenting as a girl... but *also* holding the right to refuse the girliest garments.' I found it easier to hide the extreme blushing on my face and nervously laugh it off.

"Plus with that long hair of yours, you'd make the cutest girl, wouldn't ya?" Tara added, though she took one look at my face and decided it was probably time to stop. "Okay, I'm done. I promise."

Tara stuck around for most of the day, making occasional runs back and forth from her office in the main clubhouse and the tennis stand. Thankfully for me, it was a pretty light day. There were a couple no-shows and a few cancellations due to it drizzling on and off throughout the day, and the people who did come by barely batted an eye — even with a new employee. The baggy, large white polo and shorts held up well enough, though I relied heavily on the uniform's white belt to keep me from flashing my underwear to the world.

Admittedly, I *did* wonder what the members would've said had I opted for the women's uniform. I mean, they barely paid me any mind *now* but maybe, just like the Princess Trinity followers, everyone would just assume I was a girl and move on. Something to think about for sure...

THE REST of this week was all about adjusting to the rhythm of my new responsibilities. As the wounds healed and the braces and splints either shrunk or got removed, Trinity needed less help around the house. Not that she was *healed* by any means. No no no. She still needed her sling, so she couldn't drive. And the facial bruising and broken nose — at least in *Trinity's* words — meant she was still several weeks away from being '*remotely* camera-ready'.

After such a hectic start to my tenure on Lumber Lane, it felt strange to, for once, have a little peace. Of course, Trinity's not the type of woman to sit still, so once she recognized that I had even a few stable days of work under my belt, she jumped at the opportunity to pile on a couple more things.

"Hey," she said with a coy little smile. It was a quiet afternoon that I assumed was reserved for reading my book. "You're settled, right?" Trinity took a look at my relaxed demeanor. "Yeah, you're settled. I think it's time we review a couple outfits."

I knew this would come eventually. The more mobile she became, the more antsy she got. I sighed and got up from the couch. "Alright... Whatcha got?"

"That's a good question." Trinity led me over to the pile of boxes that'd been accumulating in the laundry room. "Today we're gonna find out."

You'd think that when brands send you samples, they'd give you a little heads up that A) it's actually *coming*, and B) *what* the item is. But no, of *course* not. They send you a box and just pray you'll include it in a TikTok or IG post. To them, it's just a numbers game, but Trinity knew that game and was down to play.

So for the next 15 minutes I tore open boxes and sorted outfits, products, and accessories into 'yes's', 'maybe's', 'no's', and 'HELL no's'. To my surprise, over 50% of the items received a 'HELL no'. I guess when you have even a Princess Trinity-sized audience, you can afford to be picky.

With the sorting complete, Trinity explained that whatever we decided to feature, she wanted some full body shots — hiding my face of course.

"You've been shaving your legs, haven't you?" she asked.

I'm not sure why, but the way she said it felt like an accusation.

"Yeah, what of it?" I replied defensively, though immediately apologized. "Sorry, it's just... I've found it feels good on my sheets."

She chuckled at my immaturity. "You're so ridiculous! Hey, I'm glad you like it. Plus it gives us a ton more flexibility for outfits."

The negotiations began like a jury selection, first with no-questions-asked peremptory strikes of outfits, followed by carefully worded arguments for or against a certain look.

I held up a short, flowy babydoll sundress. "Obviously this is out. It's way too girly."

I tossed the dress aside as Trinity groaned and grabbed something new from the pile. "*Fine*. Well, I'm nixing these jeans. If your legs are shaved, we *gotta* show 'em off."

We went back and forth like this for a while until we settled on four items for me to wear that created a cohesive look. The top was a flimsy, white tunic-style blouse with butterfly sleeves. We paired my new top with tapered beige shorts and white sneakers to complete the look.

"The only question left..." Trinity began, "Do I have your approval?"

It was hard to tell before seeing myself in it. This was a tried and true *girl's* outfit — no debate there. But it could've been a *lot* worse, and both Trinity and I knew that.

"Sure," I answered. "I approve."

"Excellent," she said, smiling. But Trinity had one last addition for a convincing ensemble. "This too," she said, handing me a plain white bra. "Now go change." My eyes rolled almost to the back of my head, but I accepted the bra without debate.

I put the outfit on in the bathroom without much trouble. The shorts were shorter than expected thanks to the high-waist style and the top was so flimsy that it felt like I was wearing nothing at all. Despite its scratchiness, I understood why a bra was needed. These clothes were designed for girls with breasts after all, so a little padding not only made the top look better, but *fit* better too. It wasn't perfect, but compared to my loose, baggy work uniform, these clothes fit like a dream. Hell, I strangely pulled off the outfit. I embarrassingly gave a little spin in the mirror that *thankfully* Trinity didn't see.

"Va-va-voom!" she called out as I debuted in the living room. "You look adorable, Andie!"

I raised an eyebrow at her. "Is that the deal? I'm Andie when dressed up?"

Trinity blushed. "Well, that was my thought... But again, only if you're okay with it."

"Yeah, it's fine. Shall we take the pics?"

"Well I know your *face* won't be on camera, but your hair certainly will. The *least* I can do is run a brush through it."

I didn't object to her minimal brushing and styling, but it definitely felt a little weird sitting on the couch in a blouse, women's shorts and sneakers getting a brush run through my hair. Here I was, a 20-year-old male getting dressed up and pampered as if I were her daughter. Well, I guess in this case, her *niece*.

"Ooh, look at you!" Trinity said as she pulled back after

inserting a couple unwanted barrettes into my hair. "You're such a little darling!"

I ran over to the mirror to make sure I didn't look *too* objectionable but, sure enough, Trinity did a great job. It was a cute, simple hairstyle. My long brunette locks hung neatly just past my shoulders. Any knots or messiness were removed. And for the first time in my life, she'd created a cute middle-part — a style that's very popular, as far as I can tell.

Satisfied with the outfit and hair, Trinity took me around her house for picture-taking. Because her house has such a unique, quirky look to it, it lends itself quite nicely to photoshoots. She taught me some girly poses to make, most of which called attention to my hips and butt.

"Andie's got a bit of a booty!" she called out as I shook it for the camera. If my face *were* facing the camera, she'd see me red as a beet.

Over the next 45 minutes we must've taken over 100 pictures in five or six different locations, mixing in some video here and there. Close-ups, medium shots, full body action shots with a little dancing — Trinity wanted plenty of coverage. For the second half, she had me wear some bracelets and necklaces to showcase as well. For *that*, I had no objections. The more items we could knock out in one fell swoop, the less times I'd have to do this.

But then again, I wouldn't say I had a *bad* time... In fact, it was a lot of fun hanging out with Trinity in this regard. The clothing was pretty, I felt confident that I looked good and Trinity, while she teased me a little bit, was nothing but affirming the entire time. Not once did she make me feel like I didn't belong in these clothes, or that this cute outfit wasn't meant for my body.

Our session wrapped up with the promise to post it some-time this week.

I can't believe I'm saying this... but I'm actually looking forward to the result.

It goes without saying that I had no plans to share my dress-up escapades with anyone at work. For two main reasons.

First, despite being a 'public figure' (Trinity's words), I had no obligation to call attention to my admittedly embarrassing... hobby?... of wearing beauty products in place of my aunt. I can't imagine that would go over well with *anyone*.

But the second and main reason I wouldn't tell anybody about this at work is because, well, I don't *know* anybody else.

At this point, I'd worked only three or four shifts at the Golden Dunes tennis desk — not a *ton*, but enough where you'd think I'd be familiar with anybody else by now. But other than little friendly waves to fellow employees in the hall-way, or the wordless 'baton handoff' between shifts at the tennis desk, I haven't said more than two words to another worker.

Halfway into my shift, Tara swung by to check on me. "Well *you've* been quite lucky!"

I looked up from my textbook. Today was the first day I felt comfortable enough to actually study during the job. "Why's that?"

She gestured to the empty courts. "One of four filled? You're cruising!"

"Heh, I guess you're right..." I held up one of my notepads with scribbled words on it. "It's nice to double duty."

"It's super dead, and yet you haven't gone to the break room once," Tara added curiously, then paused to consider something. "I *did* tell you about the break room... right?"

I rolled my eyes. "Uh... *no*, Tara, you didn't!"

She slapped her forehead, embarrassed. For as kind of a woman as she was and seemingly a good manager, Tara definitely wasn't the best orienter.

"Sorry, sorry..." she conceded, glancing around to make sure no nosy members were approaching the stand. The two men at the courts were deeply engaged in their game, ignoring us anyway. "I'll show you."

Tara led me on what felt like a journey across the entire estate. It was deathly hot out today and even spending a couple minutes away from my shaded workspace made me want to push this break room trip to another day. Finally, Tara pointed to a room at the end of the hall. "Down there," she said, but was quickly interrupted by her cell phone ringing. "Shit. I gotta take this. Explore it yourself!"

I shrugged and moseyed over toward the break room alone, wondering who, if anyone, would be taking the same chance as me to escape the brutal heat. But no. Of course I wasn't lucky. Not a soul but mine was there.

The break room was simple and practical. Some couches, a kitchenette... The foosball table was a strange but thoughtful inclusion. The most notable thing about the break room was the giant floor-to-ceiling window that faces the pool. To date, this was the best look I got of the swimming area — and it was fairly impressive, especially compared to Trinity's tiny backyard one.

There were basically two sections to it. One part was a shallow, mess-around zone that tapered into something a bit deeper. The deep end mostly served as the drop zone for a wild-looking corkscrew slide. The second section was a lap pool, which I already knew about thanks to Trinity's affinity for it and self-designation as 'a regular'.

I heard chatter coming from down the hallway. A few voices, and none of them sounded like Tara. For whatever reason, I started panicking as if I wasn't supposed to be in here. I frantically spun around looking for some object to hold or food to eat — anything that'd justify my presence. But my manic anxiety didn't help.

To my surprise, three of the most gorgeous girls I'd ever seen waltzed into the room, chatting away. But the moment they saw me, they all stopped in their tracks. All three of them were in form-fitting white, one-piece swimsuits with the letters 'GDCC Lifeguard' on the front in gold letters.

I must've stared too long without saying anything, because the redhead girl in the middle addressed me. "Hey..." was all she said.

"Hi," I squeaked back, feeling two feet tall. Something about tall, attractive women always made me shrink. "I'm, uh... I'm Anderson. I work in, uh... tennis."

"Well hey, Anderson from Tennis," the cute, blonde Asian girl on the right replied. God, could I have been more awkward?

Nervously fiddling with my hair, tucking individual locks behind my ear.

The brunette girl on the left put our introductions to a halt though. "Ahh! Look!" she fervently pointed out the window toward the pool.

The girls followed her lead and sprinted to the window. I crept behind them, curious what could've spooked her. But turns out, it wasn't anything of concern. At least for *me.*

"Look what he's doing," the brunette girl swooned. Being shorter than these girls I couldn't entirely see, but it was obvious they were staring at some boy.

"What's going on?" I decided to ask after several attempts to get a view. The blonde girl moved aside for me. "Allie's got a huge crush on him."

"The Dreamsicle..." Allie, the brunette, swooned some more.

The blonde girl had clearly seen this play out before. "That's what she calls him."

Finally with a view, I could see what The Dreamsicle was actually *doing.* First of all, he was another lifeguard, evidenced by his white swim trunks and what appeared to be the same Golden Dunes logo printed on the leg. But it's not like he was juggling or performing a sick flip. He was crouched down, tossing a ball with some little kid.

"Agh, he'd be *such* a good father..." Allie revered, receiving an eye roll from the redhead girl.

I felt so silly, crowded around this window with three other girls, staring at a fellow employee. At best, this was a little creepy what we were doing. Crushes are normal, but the fact we were inside and he didn't *know* we were watching him inno-cently play with a kid felt bizarre.

Allie went on for a few more moments about how hot The Dreamsicle is, much to the annoyance of her friends.

I checked the time on my phone and realized, despite Tara's blessing, I'd left the tennis desk idle longer than I probably should have.

"Look, I gotta get go—" I began, taking a step backwards, but stepped on my loose shoelace. Instead of collapsing to the ground straight down, I made a wacky, comical attempt to keep myself upright. The three girls, suddenly agile, moved out of my way and fully let me face plant straight into the giant glass window.

"*Fuck...*" I muttered in stinging pain, but also in embarrass-ment for clownishly tripping and slamming my face in front of three pretty girls. But the girls weren't saying anything. In fact, they were tucked behind the wall, away from the window.

Well *that's* a little rude... I got myself up, basically unharmed. A little painful, but not like a Trinity-level fall.

The real scare, however, wasn't the pain from banging my face. No no no.

Staring at me, maybe 20 yards away on the pool deck, right into my eyes and *definitely* having seen the whole thing, was The Dreamsicle.

8

The smart thing would've been to duck away from the window like the other girls had. Or if not that, try to play it off like I wasn't a peeping Tom from the window, watching him innocently toss a ball with a kid. But of *course* my awkward ass did neither of those things. I just stood there like an idiot, my mouth agape and frozen from embarrassment.

The Dreamsicle looked at me a little bit longer. He stood there, his neck turned towards me but his body still facing the kid. His tanned, toned body glistened from the sunlight. Out of the corner of my eye, I could see the girls hiding behind the wall. "Is he still there??" Allie asked.

I just nodded my head, still staring at the guy. Then, in maybe the most uncomfortable, awkward way, forced a tiny, friendly wave and tiptoed out of sight.

Each of the girls' faces were in shock.

"What was that? Was he waving to you?" the blonde girl asked.

Still, I felt like a deer in headlights, almost in a daze. "I... should get back to work."

Without even saying goodbye or learning the other two girls' names, I retreated from the break room and began my walk back to the tennis courts. Thankfully my path back to the courts didn't cross the pool or maybe I'd have died of embarrassment before arriving. I'm sure right now The Dreamsicle is laughing with his friends about the weird, long-haired boy in an ill-fitting uniform peeping on him from the employee break room. Why... *Why* did I always have to be the most awkward person on the planet?

I DEBATED TELLING Trinity about the whole break room snafu. She certainly would have gotten a kick out of it. And as a pool regular, she probably *knows* all of the lifeguards. So rather than invite any haranguing, I kept that little moment secret. My first attempt to meet fellow employees was a complete disappointment and one that I had no intention of reliving.

In my defense though, I've never really been the type of person to *need* friends anyway. I operate completely fine on my own. Reading, relaxing, and helping people are what I like and do best. And all three of those things can be accomplished by maintaining the solitude status quo.

Trinity's injuries were healing up quicker and quicker it seemed. The once lethargic woman was becoming more jazzed up to cook fun meals, have deep, interesting conversations and of course, make more beauty content.

My first outfit posts performed *extremely* well on her accounts. Trinity did a really nice job editing the pictures and videos into entertaining, fair analyses of the products. All of it without showing an inch of my face. The Princess Trinity brand — at least for now — seemed to be doing just fine in the Andie era.

"We have *stellar* momentum. We gotta ride it as long as we can," Trinity reminded me one night at dinner. I found it funny how she basically turned into a football coach whenever she 'talked shop'. Though considering this content creation stuff is her *job*, it *does* make sense she'd take it so seriously.

"I mean, yes. I'm down," I said for probably the hundredth time. I think part of Trinity still couldn't believe I was willing to help her out in this manner, so she constantly felt the need to convince me to keep going. Frankly, I'm a little surprised I'm enjoying it as much as I am. However, there was one thing that kept popping into my mind each time we discussed next steps with videos.

"So all these people who follow you... Do any of them, like, *judge* you?" I asked, then rephrased my question. "Or rather, what if someone in town hates your videos? Or someone at Golden Dunes?"

Trinity was listening intently to my question, but laughed at the final part. "Oh, at *Golden Dunes?* Ha! Have you seen those people? You think they care about what *I* do?"

Well she's *way* more brazen about this than expected. "You think they don't watch?"

"Anderson, so many of those country club folks have their heads so far up their own asses, they barely know my *name*, much less what I do. I could have a million followers and they'd still want to just talk about themselves and their 'asset allocation' or 'stock buybacks' or whatever."

I took a bite of my pasta and pondered her point. Her take on the GDCC folks definitely tracked with my experiences. In fact, I don't think a single member even went out of their way to talk to me or ask for my name.

"It's an unfortunate reality, I know. And you might even call me a hypocrite for joining a club like that... But *damn* are the facilities nice!" Trinity said, chuckling. I laughed along with her. "So to answer your question? No, I don't worry about them judging me over Princess Trinity. Even if someone *did* find out and say something negative, that's not the kind of fan I want anyway."

Trinity's perspective was mature, measured, and one I aspire to share. Though it's easier said than done when *you're* the one secretly crossdressing on camera. Nonetheless, I took her inspiring message to heart.

That night, I got on the phone with my parents for only the second time since I arrived in Old Buffalo. The first time, of course, was only a day after I arrived to tell them about Trinity's fall. Our call lasted all of seven minutes.

Honestly, the call was indicative of a growing trend. I'd been drifting apart from my parents for a while now. Though the Puerto Rico decision came as somewhat of a surprise to *me*, retirement, traveling, and leaving the midwest were front of mind for so many years that I became somewhat of an afterthought, particularly after high school.

I should clarify — it's not like I hate them or they hate me. Nothing like that. It's just that when I became an adult and left the nest, the remnants of that nest blew away with the wind.

Still, Mom was polite and pleasant, telling me how they were loving the new house in Puerto Rico. My Dad shared a story about how he met some guys in their neighborhood and were starting a poker group... typical, boring parent stuff. I told them Trinity was recovering and that I found a part-time job to occupy myself and make a little money while studying for the boards. Notably I left out the Princess Trinity business, but knowing how technologically inept they are — coupled with how distant they are to Trinity — I doubt they're even aware she even *makes* content on the internet in the first place.

My parents' ignorance and apathy actually gave me internal peace in a time like this. In many ways, I'd moved on from them. They raised me, they served me well, but now it was Trinity's time to influence me. An influence I was welcoming more and more each day.

IN THE FOLLOWING WEEK, I would go on to help out Trinity not once, not twice, but *three times* for different beauty product reviews. Clearly, she wasn't kidding with this whole 'ride the momentum' thing.

The first dress-up session was much like the previous one. We had our little clothing draft to strike certain items and products that I didn't feel comfortable with, ultimately settling on another blouse and pair of shorts. Trinity had also been gifted a cute pair of sandals that she wanted to feature, so I agreed to paint my toenails a pretty shade of yellow to double-up on products. I gave my hair a healthy brushing, then Trinity styled it up into a casual, half-up half-down look, held up by a light green claw clip to match the blouse. The whole ensemble was super pretty and, I must admit, looked fantastic on me.

A few days later we upped the ante just a bit, as I agreed to wear a long, maxi skirt — my first ever skirt — paired with a cute women's tank top. The skirt was black and the tank top dark-brown, so together the pieces exuded witchy, fall energy. This was the first outfit that didn't cover my shoulders, so Trinity requested I shave my underarms for the shoot. Though hesitant at first, I understood that this would be best for concealing any perceived masculinity — even as my poses and movements became more graceful and feminine when on camera. By now I had my own shaving kit for my shower, so I took care of the remaining body hair and returned to Trinity to be dressed.

Then over the weekend, Trinity summoned me one last time for a 'swishy skirt special' planning to feature five different skirts, all by me doing a Risky Business-style slide down the hardwood floor in socks. So of course, I was given a simple girls top to pair with each of the 5 skirts and some pink girls socks that allow for ample sliding. The one unexpected request of the day, however, was that I opt out of using my boxers for the first time... and switch to panties.

I assure you that I questioned her reasoning but Trinity

convinced me that women's panties, while not the *topic* of the review, were a necessary addition to my ensemble — particularly if wearing skirts. Plus, the fact I was already accustomed to bras, panties became an easier sell. So that settled it. Some mental discomfort lingered, but it was quickly overshadowed by the surprising comfort of the underwear itself. They were simple women's control briefs that hugged my butt nicely and offered plenty of coverage. There was also just enough room to adjust my package and create a flatter-looking front without causing any pain. The socks were on, my panties secure... The rest of the shoot was smooth sailing.

"You're getting quite good at this Andie stuff," Trinity complimented as soon as we wrapped. "Even *I* find myself forgetting you're a boy sometimes."

It was hard to deny the effectiveness of these clothes. There I stood in a plain white women's tank top, a purple knee-length circle skirt, and frilly pink socks. My hair done-up in a girly, high ponytail held back with a pink scrunchie. And underneath, I comfortably wore a bra and panties. I can't speak to whether or not I'm *convincing*, but there's no doubt I've done everything in my power to look and feel as feminine as possible.

"Not that I'm pressuring you at *all*," Trinity began, "But you know... makeup would suit you quite nicely. And I haven't been able to review any of that since all... *this*." She gestured to her face — healing, but not without its visible bruising.

It was a clever use of flattery and guilt, but my desire for anonymity stayed strong — at least for today. "Maybe another time," I told her.

Though as I disrobed and changed back into my boy clothes for the day, I couldn't help but feel like I was shedding a little bit of joy in the process. I liked looking good. I liked look-ing... *cute*.

THE BRIEF BOUT of confidence I had when taking pictures and filming content for Princess Trinity never seemed to last when-ever I arrived at Golden Dunes. Not that I hate the job by any means, but something about the folks there and the odd power dynamic always kept me on edge. Just as Trinity had described, the people here weren't cruel or immoral. Just... *above* everyone else. Many members held an air of superiority that created this intangible, invisible classist wall. I tried not to let that bother me, and for the most part, I did a good job of that. Mostly because I had enough other reasons to be anxious.

It's been over a week since my awkward break room issue. The lifeguard girls, The Dreamsicle... I couldn't get any of that out of my mind. Why is it that whenever I try to branch out and meet people that I end up looking like a complete idiot?

So of course, I avoided the break room like the plague. The tennis courts being on the opposite side of campus provided a buffer of comfort. Though, at least *so far*, I haven't been handed a restraining order against anyone, or forced to wear a name tag that read 'CREEPY' or 'AWKWARD'.

The one good piece of news was that Trinity had ordered a proper 'small' size uniform for me, so I was *finally* able to walk around campus not looking like a baggy-clothed weirdo.

The country club job, my increasing involvement with Princess Trinity, and the looming fear that I'm not doing enough to be properly prepared for the boards exam was starting to get to me. Additionally, Trinity had a slight setback when trying to lift something using her bad arm. It was a harsh reminder that despite what seemed like rapid progress, injuries take a *long* time to heal.

Even worse, the setback noticeably dampened Trinity's mood. More time was spent alone in her room or on the couch rather than her typical 'let's get up and do something!' attitude. God, I hated seeing her down... For someone who had become such a motivational influence on me, I felt like I was experiencing second-hand depression. I had to do something about it.

"Trinity?" I called out, gently knocking on her door. It was mid-day and unlike her to not be out and about.

"Yeah, one sec..." she replied groggily. Shit. I must've woken her up from a nap. But ever the positive one, Trinity opened her door with a sleepy smile.

"Sorry if I caught you mid nap, but I was thinking... Hey, we got nothing going on today. Wanna review a couple Princess Trinity products?"

Either due to pain or disinterest, Trinity hadn't even *floated* the idea of making content for several days. So the fact *I* was the one bringing it up brought a genuinely warm smile to her face.

"Really?" she asked, not quite believing me.

"Sure! Whatever you wanna do, I'll do."

Immediately I could see the gears turning in her head, mentally sifting through her backlog of unreviewed products. "Hmm... Well, a lot of the stuff we got left is pretty girly..."

I nervously bit my lip. To date, I've avoided the super girly, *super* feminine items. But Trinity needed a pick-me-up more than anything right now. "I guess that's fine…"

Her face lit up, "Oh my God, *really?* Ah! Let me put together something for you!"

Trinity was so excited she practically shoved me aside as she raced to the closet of gifted clothing. I stood back, revering her enthusiasm but fearing what she might pick. It didn't take long for her to settle on — of *course* — a dress.

"This'll look darling on you," Trinity said, holding it up against my body. Of all the things she presented me to date, this was easily the girliest thing. It was a yellow sundress with poofy sleeves, a scooped neckline, and a skirt that went just past my knees. The soft, delicate fabric was speckled with little white daisies. It was flowery, summery, and feminine as hell.

"Okay…" I said through gritted teeth. "It's… Well, it's pretty."

"Damn right it is!" Trinity said confidently. "That white bra and panties set you've been wearing should be good for this…" Trinity looked overwhelmed, spinning around and searching for more product options to pair with her dress decision. "Uhh… You know what? I'll be able to focus better if I hop in the shower first. Put this on and give me 10, okay?"

Her chaotic energy might've been a little imposing, but I'd take it over her depressive state any day. Because of that, I was more than happy to put on the dress. With Trinity tucked away in her room, I changed out in the living room. I was accustomed to the bra, I was accustomed to the panties, but the dress was a whole new thing. Fit-wise, it felt similar to the skirt — loose, fun, and flowy. But unlike the skirt, the dress required a tricky maneuver to zip it up in the back. I struggled, twisting my body and arms to get that damned zipper up, but it wasn't working. I figured I'd just wait for Trinity's help once she's done in the shower.

There I sat in the living room, hearing the rush of water from down the hall in her bathroom. I thought about how far I'd come since that first night painting my nails with her, nervously shaving my legs for the first time in her bathroom. At that point, the only Princess Trinity-related experience I'd had was that brief moment she put lipstick on me. And now? Well, I'm waiting patiently, like a proper lady, to have my sundress zipped up and my hair styled like a girl.

I could hear the water shut off from down the hall — the walls weren't especially thick after all.

DING!

Trinity's feet clomped from across the house. "Crap! Hey Andie, if you can hear me, can you get that?"

Answering the door was obviously *not* ideal, considering I was half-dressed — not to mention wearing *girls* clothes. I didn't have a perfect view of the front door, but I saw the outline of a figure standing there.

"Uhh, who are you expecting?"

"I asked Kelly to come over to do a few things around the yard."

I paused. "Who's Kelly?"

"A lifeguard at the club. Just answer it, will you?"

SHIT. Are you kidding me? I'd already embarrassed myself enough in front of those girls a week ago, and now one of them was at the door, about to see me in a dress? And not just *in a* dress, but *unzipped* in a dress. One unfortunate snag or body turn could have this dress toppling to the floor. But despite my fear, I took a deep breath and walked toward the front door.

I'd actually been wondering all week which girl was which. At the moment, all I knew was that Allie's the brunette. The blonde and the redhead were still a mystery. Of course, there could be more lifeguards that *weren't* those three — but would that really make things any better? I imagine that word of a dress-wearing male colleague would spread fast anyway. I tried not to look through the glass of the door and answered it as confidently as possible. Just put on a brave face...

I closed my eyes as I swung open the door. "Here to see Trinity?"

"Uh... yeah. She called me over," the person said. But it *wasn't* a girl's voice. It was male.

'Fuck my life' was my genuine, immediate thought. I didn't even need to open my eyes to know who it was. With the kind of luck I've had this past month or so, it could *only* be one person. But when I finally peeked, my suspicions were confirmed. Sure enough it was him, standing right in front of me.

The Dreamsicle.

9

If there was any silver lining, it's that he *already* must think I'm a creep after catching me staring. Granted, wearing a dress, I could get lucky and he'd just *assume* I'm someone else.

"You're Kelly?" I asked, raising my voice just a tad into the feminine register. Was I trying to be a girl? Was I trying to just sound different? I was merely flying by the seat of my pants. Or, uh... my *dress*.

Kelly stood there, looking at me like I asked the dumbest question ever. "Were you not expecting me?"

"No, we were," I said, letting him step inside, though not shifting my body too much to keep the dress from falling. "Trinity will be out in a second."

The two of us stood there, awkwardly for a moment. Before now, I'd only seen Kelly at a distance. I hadn't even heard his *voice*. But he was just as expected. He was tall. Like, *very* tall — maybe

6'4 or 6'5. He had broad shoulders, toned arms, and an overall fit physique that I got full view of when I saw him shirtless at the pool the other week. His brunette hair was short and neat, messed up with a bit of product. While his body was that of a late-20s male athlete, he had a boyish, youthful face that confirmed he was probably around my age, or at least in his early 20s.

Kelly looked down at me, smirking a little at my discomfort. "Need a little help there?"

I stood next to him, still, afraid that my dress would fall to the ground and I'd embarrass myself even further. "No. I'm fine," I answered curtly.

"Okay. It's just that it's falling off your shoulders. I have a sister. I know how to zip up a dress."

I glared at him, frustrated that he was even referencing my outfit. But he was right. "Sure, go for it."

Kelly swiftly reached behind me and zipped up the dress to completion. It was now snug and secure around my back.

"Thank you," I replied, not sure what to say further. I still had no idea if this guy even knew who I was. *Does* he remember our incident? Does he even think I'm a boy?

I heard Trinity's door open from down the hall and she rushed out to save the day. "Kelly, hi!" She greeted him warmly but was quickly distracted by how vivacious the dress looked on me. "Oh... *Wow*! Kelly, have you met..."

"Andie," I interrupted her with my slightly higher-pitched voice. I guess in the meantime I'd decided to play off being a girl.

Trinity raised her eyebrow at my feminine introduction but

nonetheless rolled with it. "*Andie*," she said. "Mind if I walk Kelly through some of the yard work I need done? You just keep getting pretty for our shoot, okay?"

I nodded and let the two of them walk back outside for instruction. When the door finally shut I let out a huge sigh of... well, not *relief* but exasperation. Other than Trinity, Kelly was the first person to see me in girls clothes *in person*. Can you blame me for being nervous? There's not exactly a handbook on how to handle these types of situations.

With my bra, panties, and dress all on, there wasn't much to do but wait for Trinity to come back inside.

"*Well?*" Trinity shot at me the second the door closed. "You're going by Andie now??"

I stood up, furious. "It's not like I had a choice! That's... That guy works at the pool!"

Trinity nodded, well aware of his employment. "I know. He's a lifeguard. I swim there all the time, remember?"

"But why... *him?*" I grumbled. "We had a, uh... a run-in."

I briefly filled in Trinity on the situation with the break room window and the accidental creeping. You'd think with the way I told the story she'd gasp and immediately apologize. But no. She just laughed.

"Ha! Are you kidding me? That's not *creeping*, Andie. I know Kelly, he wouldn't care."

"Well... Maybe not. But now everything's just so, I dunno... *awkward*. So I panicked and just pretended to be a girl."

Trinity sighed, not sure what she was supposed to do here. "Look, handle this however you want, but I promise he'd be chill about it." She paced the room and eyed her ring light. "Maybe some pictures will take your mind off this."

I sighed. "Yeah, maybe. Alright, what do you need?"

It wasn't easy getting Kelly out of my mind, but Trinity did everything in her power to keep things light. Thankfully, I had no view of Kelly as he was out working in the garden, so I wouldn't feel so watched while jumping and prancing around in this dress.

My initial offer to go 'all out' was taken full advantage of my Trinity. While we still didn't do anything to my face, Trinity gave me 'the works' everywhere else. Already in a bra, panties, and this yellow, flowery sundress, I was subsequently given a cute, girlish hairstyle of a half-up fishtail braid, accented with a cute, beige bandana.

While Trinity styled my hair, I painted each nail on my fingers and toes a light, summer orange that looked nice along-side the dress. While the nails dried, we sifted through necklace and bracelet options and discussed which pair of sandals I should wear. Soon enough, all of the dressing was done and I looked completely and utterly like a girl.

"I told you, you've got potential," Trinity praised as I spun around in the mirror.

"You're the mastermind," I said. "It's all smoke and mirrors."

Over the next half-hour we took pictures and videos of me posing and prancing around in the cute outfit. Some inside, some outside — though I insisted we stick to the front yard to keep as far a distance from Kelly as possible. Trinity even had the cute idea of me holding a picnic basket and skipping merrily down the road. As strange as it seems, I was genuinely enjoying the shoot. The clothing was light and airy and my hair felt marvelous bouncing around my shoulders and brushing my back.

Once our shoot was complete, Trinity suggested we go back inside and have some lemonade to celebrate.

"*Damn* it's hot," she grieved, wiping sweat from her brow. "I freaking hate these heat waves."

She wasn't wrong. Even *standing* out in the hot sun I was starting to sweat. If I'd skipped around any longer than our two takes, I'd probably be drenched. Then I thought about Kelly, who was working in the unshaded garden. I craned my neck to see if he was in view from the kitchen.

"You're not gonna see him," Trinity said. "Garden's pretty secluded. That's one issue I have with this property... I got this beautiful space for a garden and it's all the way in the back out of view." Trinity lamented, then sipped her lemonade. "Here's an idea. How about you bring Kelly a glass?"

I paused mid-sip. "Like... like *this*?" I asked, referring to my full girl-mode outfit.

"Why not?" Trinity shrugged. "If he already thinks you're a girl, go out there as a girl."

The thought of confronting him at all was terrifying, even more so in this outfit. But she did have a point. This 'I'm a girl named Andie' stuff might not be sustainable in the long term, but it's an effective punt.

"Alright," I decided, though I had *one* more request for a little boost of confidence. "But before I go out... should I maybe wear a little bit of makeup?"

Trinity looked at me, floored. "You *want* to wear makeup?"

She nearly spit out her lemonade. "I mean, yes! I'd love to put some on you."

Her enthusiasm almost made me take back my request, but I carried forward with it. "Just so I'm a little bit more convincing, okay? Don't go too hard!"

She practically squealed as she shot up from her seat and went to fetch her products. "Anything you want, Andie! Eeeee!"

Before doing anything, she had me rid my face of any oil and sweat by giving it a quick wash. When I returned from the bathroom, she was ready with some simple products.

"Mascara's a must for any girl," she explained, delicately brushing my lashes with the dainty black brush. "It makes your eyes pop!"

Trinity went on to apply some concealer around my eyes, some light powder, and topped me off with a fruity-tasting, pink lipgloss. Lipgloss which I immediately started tasting.

"It may be yummy, but it's for show, remember?" Trinity reminded me. I nodded as she reapplied a fresh layer.

She led me back to the mirror for the reveal and, I'll say, it was the perfect amount of change. I looked objectively prettier (not to mention more convincingly female), but not in a 'night on the town' glam kind of way. It was subtle, cute, and gave me the perfect amount of poise.

With my confidence and outfit as solid as they're gonna get, I poured some lemonade into an ice-filled glass and bravely went outside to deliver it to Kelly.

The heat was intense. Even with no exertion and wearing a light, airy dress I was starting to sweat. So I couldn't imagine what poor Kelly was going through. Past the pool and back into the garden, I finally got my answer.

There he was — Kelly, the Dreamsicle — hedge clippers in hand and trimming away... shirtless, with only athletic shorts, sunglasses, and bulky headphones on. Just like at the pool, Kelly's tanned muscular upper body glistened in the heat of the sun. And there *I* stood, the same 20 or so yards away, watching him from the exact opposite side of the masculinity spectrum. I'd learned my lesson to *not* get caught staring, so I shouted his name loudly until he heard me through the music playing in his headphones.

"Brought you some lemonade" I said bluntly, a little peeved that it took this long for him to notice.

Kelly paused, put down his hedge clippers and wiped his brow. He looked me over for a moment, then gave that same little smirk from earlier. "What's this little waitress bit Trinity's got you doing, huh?"

What? I turned red on the spot, though it was hard to tell in the bright sunlight. "Umm... *what* are you talking about?" I answered, not entirely sure if he was joking or being serious. His tone was so dry that it was impossible to tell.

"I dunno, just this dress, the little bandana in your hair... Bringing me *lemonade*..."

"It's for a video!" I fumed. "Not everything's about you." I wasn't sure if snapping back at him was the appropriate response, but it felt right in the moment.

Kelly held up his hands in concession. "Alright, alright... it's for a video. Lighten up."

The frustrating man didn't deserve an explanation, but

something about standing there in a little sundress with my hair and makeup done put me on the immediate defensive. "I'm actually studying to be a nurse, you know."

He nodded stoically. "Cool, cool... and the waitress dress-up videos help with your work... how?"

"THEY'RE NOT WAITRESS VIDEOS!" I yelled at him, but his tiny smirk suggested he was yanking my chain. I cooled down for a second. "What's your problem?"

"I'm sorry, okay? I'm just kidding." Finally Kelly stepped forward and took the lemonade from my hand. He removed his sunglasses and wiped his brow again before taking a sip. "Thank you for this," he said earnestly.

Surprised by his sudden sincerity, I squeaked out a 'your welcome'.

"Can you tell Trinity I've got about a half hour left? Then I promise to be out of your hair."

Fine by me. I'd had enough of this guy and his needling for one day. I simply nodded and walked back to the house.

"Or rather," Kelly added, just before putting his head-phones back on. "Until the next time you inevitably stare at me from the break room, Anderson."

I stopped in my tracks and whipped around toward him, but he'd already put his headphones back on. I tried to get his attention but he merely mouthed 'I can't hear you', flashing that same teasing smirk. He gestured to his headphones as got back to work.

Ugh! What the fuck is this guy's *problem*?

WELL HIS LAST words all but proved it. Kelly didn't just know I was a boy, but he knew I was *the* boy from the break room window. He knew I was staring at him — even thought it meant *nothing*! — and he had full knowledge of the fact I work with my aunt to make girly dress up videos. Fan-fucking-*tastic*...

I shared the details of my Kelly interaction with Trinity, though she didn't provide much relief. She mostly giggled at my story and found Kelly's annoying attempts at 'humor' to be 'charming'. However, she did insist that I shouldn't worry about word getting out about my involvement with Princess Trinity.

"Seriously... People at that club really don't give a shit about others," she reminded me. I guess that *kinda* helps.

Kelly aside, the big takeaway from the weekend was how freaking stellar I apparently look in a sundress. I mean *damn*! Trinity showed me the pictures and I simply couldn't believe it was me. The bra, panties, dress, sandals... everything fit like a dream and came out great on camera. My first ever braid held up great and looked adorable paired with the bandana. And my *butt*? Jesus! Something about the fit of the sundress gave the illusion that I had wide hips and a perky little tush. Combined with the padded bra, I had a serious figure.

If you'd asked me before, I would've bet a thousand dollars that the dress would be my final straw and a step too far. But the result was the opposite. Instead of reverting to my previously careless, masculine-ish standards of hygiene, I opted to continue shaving my legs and underarms. I started moisturizing more, and had Trinity help me develop a nighttime skincare routine. I not only more frequently brushed my hair, but added oils and conditioners to it so it would be healthier and softer than ever before.

But of course, this was only at home. After all, I had a reputation to uphold at the club. Tara always insisted that 'clean-cut with a smile' was the way to go, and it was a standard I noticed was followed by employees in every department — even if I'd been actively avoiding others for the past week.

Despite my best efforts, I *do* still run into other GDCC employees at the tennis courts. It isn't and has never been *only* me working there. From what I can tell, there are three other attendant stand employees who fill in the shifts throughout the week. One is a boy named Nathan whose Dad belongs to the club. Then there are the Velmahos twins, a boy and a girl a year or two younger than me who, you guessed it, *also* have a parent that belongs to the club. But other than a courteous nod or small bit of conversation, I barely know these people.

The other employees — which *aren't* full-time — are a handful of tennis instructors who filter in throughout the week. Golden Dunes itself has no full-time tennis instructor, instead opting for freelance coaches who have some side deal with the club to give private or small-group lessons. Greg, Laurie, and Addison are their names, and if I thought the other *attendants* were dismissive of me, the coaches were that times 100. They show up to the court, give me as much as a nod of acknowledgement, then teach their lesson and leave.

Does the constant dismissiveness drive me insane? At this point, I've just gotten used to it. This is a club *for* elites and, in many cases, *run* by elites too. My employment here is merely a means to an end. Which is why Tara's request toward the end of my Wednesday afternoon was... let's say, unexpected.

"What're you doing now?" Tara spat out frantically, scaring me. The courts were quiet, so I was taking the opportunity to study.

"Nothing. Studying. What's up?"

"You played tennis in high school, right?"

What was she getting at? "Um... yeah? Just JV though." I glanced at the four empty courts in front of me. "Are you trying to get some games in?"

She shook her head. "Ha! Never! But seriously, Addison just texted me and said she broke her collarbone."

"Oh my *God*... Is she okay?" I asked, concerned.

Tara shrugged. "I assume so, if she can send a text."

I looked at the court schedule for the day. Addison's name was slotted for the next hour. "So she can't run the next lesson?"

"The next or maybe *any* lesson for a while... Greg and Laurie are busy for the day, so I was hoping..."

I now knew where Tara was headed with this. "You want *me* to coach? Tara, I haven't played in like a year. And I only ever coached 5-year-olds at a summer camp *once*."

Tara swatted at the air dismissively. "Oh, I know you'll be fine. I trust you completely." She then leaned in for a whisper despite nobody being around. "Plus, it's this woman's first lesson ever. She'll never know the difference!"

That certainly felt like a lot of pressure being someone's introduction to the sport of tennis. Once again, I felt like my goodwill was being stretched further, but with the courts empty and Tara in a real pickle, I think it made sense to oblige just this once.

"Alright, I'll do it," I told her. I glanced down at my shoes. While I finally had a uniform that *fit* me, it wasn't appropriate for active play. "You got a spare instructor uniform?"

Tara bit her lip awkwardly. I felt another request coming... But it wasn't even a *request*. It was an anticipated demand. Tara had a bag beside her feet.

"See, I figured you'd say yes... And you're *always* so down to lend a hand. But I was hoping — especially with how fluid you are with clothing..." Tara reached into the bag. "...that you'd be okay if we only had women's uniforms left?"

10

I t wasn't the request itself that threw me. While I did keep finding myself in situations that required feminine clothing, I didn't really mind *wearing* it. What concerned me was Tara's cavalier attitude and assumption that I'm 'fluid with clothing'.

"Have you been watching my Aunt's videos?" I asked her, immediately on the defensive.

"Of course I do. I'm *friends* with Trinity." Tara sounded honest, though a little thrown off my accusatory tone. "If you're concerned about others seeing you in a skirt, I totally get it."

Again, Tara was missing the issue. "The others — like, everyone *else* at the club — they don't know about the videos, do they?"

"The Princess Trinity stuff? Not a chance. Again, Anderson, if you haven't realized by now, nobody really gives a shit about others around here." Sensing my hesitance and frustration,

Tara came up beside me and placed her hand on my shoulder. "We're here to do a job. One that we should all take seriously, but should never let affect us too much. If wearing a skirt and teaching a tennis lesson is too much, then I'll tell the member we're canceling on her."

"No. I'll do it," I answered confidently. "You're right. I shouldn't care about what people think of me. Public or private, I'm doing what I want."

She smiled warmly like a proud mentor. "That's the right attitude! Go in the back room and change. I'll direct Janice to the courts."

I took the bag from her and went into the storage portion of the attendant shack to change. The uniform wasn't unfamiliar to me as I'd seen it on several women before. Maybe I should be embarrassed, but I had no issues slipping on the skirt, socks, tight t-shirt, and athletic shoes. I'd certainly done it enough by now. The bag also had a golden scrunchie inside which I used to put my hair into a cute, flirty high ponytail.

Even without makeup, to an outside observer, there was nothing about my appearance that read 'male'. I couldn't help but wonder how Trinity was introducing me to the woman, Janice. Would she assume I'm female? I certainly can't keep up a female voice for an entire lesson. The next hour would boil down to how accepting this woman is.

"Anderson, you ready?" I heard Tara call from outside. Well, the fact I'm being called 'Anderson' says I won't need to hide anything. I bravely stepped out and revealed my cute uniform to...

"I know *you*..." the woman said, almost immediately. I froze in my tracks. Next to Tara stood a woman in her mid-50s. It took a second, but she looked strangely familiar too.

"The woman wagged her finger at me, as if that helped her recall past memories. "Yes! You were in the hospital a bit ago. You came to see your Auntie!"

Holy *shit*. Now I recognized her. She was the receptionist on the hospital floor that led me to Trinity's hospital room. That was only my second day in Old Buffalo. So much had happened since then, my memory of her had almost completely faded.

"Oh, uh, hello!" I answered. "Yes! That was me."

Janice grinned, glancing at my outfit. "*You've* certainly changed. Not that it's a bad look!" Her tone was more teasing than judgmental, thankfully. She was undoubtedly a little kooky, but kooky I can totally handle.

"Well, we were out of men's uniforms, so I had to improvise. Hope I look okay!" I replied cheerfully, remembering that Janice was still a member and I needed to treat her with a certain level of distance and respect. "But you're here to learn tennis! So, shall we?"

Janice and I took the court as I racked my brain for any drill I could remember from my high school days. But it was completely unnecessary because Tara wasn't kidding — Janice was a *true* beginner, evidenced by the fact she could barely hold a racket the correct way. But baby steps were fine for me, because in many ways with my feminine presentation, I was doing just the same.

Objectively, the lesson was a bit of a shit show. *Neither* of us really knew what we were doing. I almost always explained the concepts poorly, and the few times *I* did well, Janice couldn't execute. But I never got too stressed, mostly because Janice was such a calming, patient person. That fact, out of everything, was what surprised me the most. A member who not only cared to look me in the eye, but was patient and delightful to be around? What a concept!

Though I didn't ask, I assumed Janice's husband was a local hotshot, as most of the women were. After all, I can't imagine a hospital receptionist position pays well enough to get private tennis lessons, not to mention being a member at Golden Dunes. But neither her money nor ego were ever flaunted, and when the lesson came to an end, I felt I owed her an apology.

"Look, I really hope you got something out of this," I said as she packed up her things and sipped on water. "I'm not sure if Tara told you, but... I'm not actually a *real* instructor."

Janice chuckled. "Is that so? I couldn't tell," she said with a playful sarcasm, flashing me a wink. "I'm barely even a real student. I only really come here because my husband loves the golf course so much. But I appreciate your patience with me today. I feel I got better working with you."

Whether she was being honest or just making me feel better, I took the compliment.

"Let's get another one of these on the books... *if* that's alright with you," Janice pulled out her wallet and handed me a crisp $100 bill.

My eyes grew wide at the gesture. "Oh my gosh, I can't accept that... I was just covering."

But Janice shoved the bill into my palm and closed it. "I insist. Call it a tip."

I was practically melting from her generosity but tried to

play it cool. "Fine, a few more lessons then. But if you're gonna pay me, please do it through Tara. I don't wanna seem shifty."

Janice gushed at my gesture. "And an honorable one too! You'd be quite the catch," she added with a wink.

She was all smiles as I walked her to the exit gate. While I reached in for a professional handshake, Janice instead leaned in for a hug. I couldn't believe the impact I'd made on this woman, all from one, loosely thrown-together tennis lesson.

"Can I just say one more thing? You move so gracefully in that outfit," Janice declared before leaving. So twirled a short strand of hair from her short bob-cut. "I promised myself I wouldn't ask if this was your first time in a skirt, but regardless, please don't make it your last. You look *stunning*."

I helplessly blushed at her kind words, thanking her as she walked away. There's no way she knew about Princess Trinity. But even if she did, the 'secret' that I sometimes wore feminine things was about as public as it could be.

I stood there alone, swishing my skirt back and forth, mesmerized by the adorable little sway of the fabric. Maybe she had a point. Maybe I *should* be wearing this stuff out more often...

To absolutely nobody's surprise, Trinity was *ecstatic* that I taught a full, hour-long lesson in a women's tennis uniform.

"Gah!! You see? I *told* you these clothes were meant for you! Now if only we had pictures for Princess Trinity..."

I quickly assured her that any work-related dressing was to

stay entirely separate from my work with Princess Trinity. Not that I was inherently embarrassed by either. Clearly not if I'm doing this in public. But the last thing I needed was to actively inform my coworkers of the girly side project. Both Tara and Kelly being privy was already enough.

By now it had been over a week since I laid eyes on Kelly. Trinity hadn't summoned him to Lumber Lane for yard work, and I actively avoided running into him at the club. Trinity, not understanding how much he annoyed me, dared to suggest I swing by the pool for a hello and to 'make friends'. Not a *chance*! I certainly didn't want to and if *he* did, he would've come over to the courts by now. I really tried to not think about him. All it ever did was get me riled up and annoyed.

With our increasingly busy schedules, Trinity and I were having more trouble fitting in planned movie nights. But things lined up just right for a Friday movie night in, complete with snacks and wine. I even let Trinity talk me into these at-home pedicure kits she got in the mail.

"No promises it'll be good, but it'll be something to do during the movie," she assured. "Oh! I forgot to show you something."

Trinity grabbed her laptop and I watched her log in to her TikTok business account. She'd shown me this before. It outlines reach, engagement, and all the marketing mumbo-jumbo that *she* loved to keep track of but I found a little over-whelming. I've never been a huge charts-and-graphs kinda person anyway. But the graph she pulled up immediately caught my eye.

"See this trend line?" she traced it on the screen with her

finger, all the way to the end when the height of the line tripled or maybe quadrupled. "Our last post *blew* up!"

"Holy shit..." I muttered, still in shock from the reveal. "Which post was it?"

"The one of you skipping, of course. Your *favorite.*" Trinity loved teasing me about the excessively girly posts. Even though they were objectively less of a hassle as of late. "Our follower count took a huge jump too. I feel like we need to celebrate! Down for ice cream before the movie?"

Who was I to deny some free ice cream? I enthusiastically accepted and ran to throw on my shoes. But Trinity held back for a moment.

"You know, we *are* celebrating *Andie's* success... aren't we?" Trinity had that sly look on her face I'd gotten so accustomed to. "Think maybe *she* could join me out to celebrate?"

I paused before putting on my shoes. "You think people would care?"

"Care about what? That you look pretty? No, I don't think they'll care."

I'd actually wondered about that in the few days since my tennis lesson. I was nervous about wearing a skirt in front of Janice, but everything went well. Wearing the dress on camera was a *huge* step out of my comfort zone... but people loved my look more than ever. Maybe this was the opportunity I was waiting for. Tonight can be a celebration not just of this one post, but of how far I've come in my personal confidence.

"Let's do it," I declared with authority. "What should I wear?"

In classic Trinity fashion, she already had an entire outfit and style in mind for me. No longer chained by a femininity limit, Trinity had full permission to dress me in almost anything — barring it wasn't *too* revealing. Though I handed her the reins, I think we *both* knew of my growing favor toward skirts. Being a chillier summer evening, she dressed me in a cute oversized beige sweater that was so long on me it nearly covered up the short, dark green pleated skirt. Afraid my legs would get too cold, Trinity gave me thigh-high socks to wear for a combination of warmth and style. Embracing the spontaneous, autumn energy of my look, Trinity accessorized with a thick brown headband that just screamed 'girl-next-door'. Lastly, she added some light mascara for that extra, girlish touch, and my look was complete.

"God... How the hell do you look so fucking cute in literally *everything*, Andie?"

I smiled sweetly as I accepted her compliment. Though I didn't say anything, I did notice her call me 'Andie', despite this not being an official Princess Trinity shoot.

Dressed and ready to go, I drove us over to MooMoo Ice Cream, a popular spot for treats in Old Buffalo. Tonight was no exception as the place was flooded with a mix of tourists and locals.

MooMoo's specialty — besides their delicious ice cream — was the wall-to-wall cow memorabilia. Cow pictures, cow clocks, little stuffed cows, goofy utter-themed t-shirts... it's a unique vibe, but people seem to love it. There was even a giant, cartoon cow mascot on the sign out-front obnoxiously greeting customers and passers-by alike.

I felt a little nervous exiting the car and approaching the

shop. Until now, a total of four people had seen me dressed in girls clothes *in person* — and only 3 of those 4 encounters went well. But tonight I was opening myself to the judgment of nearly a hundred people, all strangers.

The level of confidence I had at the house was not the same once we got out of the car. Trinity could tell I was nervous and calmly held my shoulder to ease my nerves. My fear was that I'd be stared at and mocked. But only *half* of that was true. Yes, I got some looks... but *none* of them seemed immediately judgmental. In fact, as we waited in the packed line, surrounded by bovine beauty, I noticed the same person peeking at me multiple times.

"See that guy over there?" I whispered to Trinity, referencing a teenage boy a few places ahead of us in line. "He keeps looking over."

She smiled and shook her head. "Well aren't you sweet... Have you considered he might be checking you out? He probably thinks you're cute."

Hmm... Trinity was probably right. I felt a little silly not immediately realizing, but can you blame me? I've never looked 'cute' in public before, so therefore no reason for guys to look at me. It felt... *strange*. Validating, sure. But strange...

That boy wasn't the only one either. In the ten minutes we spent waiting, I noticed at least four other boys glance at me with that same 'interested' look. In what felt like an out-of-body moment, I even made a tiny wave to one of them. Though my gesture was interrupted by Trinity shoving me toward the register.

"Just go order, Juliet..." she teased. "*Romeo* will be there for you later..."

"I'm *not* talking to him!" I spat out through gritted-teeth, deathly embarrassed that she said that out loud.

Unfortunately for me, the employee that took my order was *also* making eyes at me. He was a tall, handsome 20-something with a beard — definitely a few years older than me, but that didn't stop him from flirting.

"What can I get ya?" he asked with a smile. A normal question, yes, but the *way* he asked it was just... *different*. I honestly didn't mean to do it, but as I ordered, I instinctively matched his flirtatious tone.

"How's the mint chocolate chip?"

"*All* the girls love it," he answered. "Especially the cute ones."

I smirked. "Well now I *have* to get it, don't I?"

We shared a laugh as he served me my scoop.

The interaction was a brief, meaningless one that definitely shouldn't be overreacted to. A boy flirted with me and I *kinda* flirted back. So what? People flirt. Flirting can be *fun*, but it really *is* meaningless. Flirting with a guy as Andie holds no bearing on if *Anderson* is interested in guys.

Though I tried not to read into it too deeply and just go with the flow, I couldn't help but notice a certain look in Trinity's eye. The kind of look she made when she was coming up with an idea.

"You look like you're planning something," I told her on the ride home. "What's going on?"

"Oh.... nothing..." she answered casually. "Nothing at all..."

11

If there's one thing I've just *barely* begun to scratch the surface of, it's the implementation of a healthy, balanced life — and the realization of how freaking impossible that can be.

I think about high school often, when things were so much simpler. Now sure, it was stressful at times — classes, homework, athletics, clubs... all of that. The days were packed, but the stakes were always low. I mean, who cares if you got a D in History Freshman year? Or Jimmy in third period said a mean thing to you in passing? Like, he's probably a loser anyway and it has *zero* bearing on your future. No individual moment affects your future too significantly. And that's important to recognize.

Even community college nursing school, all things considered, made for a simple, straightforward life. Wake up, go to class, come home to read or play video games, go to bed. Rinse and repeat. I didn't *have* to think about my career on a day-today basis. Hell, I barely even thought about *myself* or the things I wanted or liked.

But along came summer and, for the first time, I felt like I'd been thrown in the deep end, forced to swim on my own. Studying for the NCLEX I expected, but balancing a country club job with being the workhorse / live-in helper for my injured aunt added a whole other overwhelming element. Not to mention helping out with her videos — a task that grew more and more consuming. Of course, I was happy to do all of this and more. Work is a part of growing up. So why do I feel so... I don't know... held back?

I'd have to be blind to not realize the feminine changes I've made this summer. The boy who once scoffed at the idea of even trying on lipstick was now shaving his entire body, taking care of his long hair, and wearing skirts in public. While at times a few things felt like a step too far, I've mostly embraced these changes and willingly furthered them. This 'new version' of me... I kind of like it. But I can't help but wonder if it's all too good to be true. Can someone like myself with an ever-growing tower of duties and responsibilities really justify personal experimentation? Is it maybe a bit reckless?

These thoughts kept me up at night not just tonight but the whole week. Hell, if Trinity weren't so constantly positive, I'd have probably crumbled under the pressure a month ago. Trinity, genuinely, is a superstar. The legacy she's built, the outlook she has on life — all of it — is just so impressive. Sometimes I just look at her and think... 'how did she do this all alone?'

"Anderson, come here!" Trinity called from downstairs, interrupting another mind-spiraling session. *Thankfully.*

I came downstairs and turned the corner to a deeply shocking, nearly unprecedented sight. Trinity had a full face of makeup.

"Oh... Oh my *God...*" I stammered, trying to think of the last time my aunt looked this good. Her swelling and bruising had been improving for weeks, and while there had been good days and bad, on the whole, she's been looking much closer to normal. But *with* makeup? I'd say she looked 95% as I saw her the first time.

"Nice, right?" She smiled with a little twirl, still being careful not to move her shoulder too much. "It's my first time putting on a full face since the accident."

Always the on-duty guru, she felt obligated to give me a full walkthrough of the products, everything from foundation and mascara to products I'd never even *heard* of before, much less tried on, like fancy primers and blending tools. Seeing Trinity in a full face of makeup reminded me how stunningly beautiful she was. She was in her 40s but could easily pass for late-20s in the right outfit.

"So what's this for?" I asked, grabbing a lemonade from the fridge. "Someone invite you to a party?"

"Oh, no no no... No parties for me. But I was thinking about making a triumphant return to the club, you know? With the big night?"

I paused for a moment, then slapped my head having foolishly forgotten it was the Fourth of July. There were flyers freakin' *everywhere* around the club, promoting the Pig Roast and fireworks show. Though as a couple of vegetarians, we'd ignore the former in favor of the latter.

Trinity motioned for me to grab a can of soda. She cracked it and sipped. "We should go. You and me. It'll be a fun night out! Plus, you can finally meet some non-tennis people."

Seeing her jazzed up to hit the town warmed my heart — even if 'the town' was a family-friendly evening at her country club.

"Let's do it!" I smiled, admiring Trinity's beaming confidence even more than her beauty. Was I feeling my best as of late? Definitely not. But just because I was an introspective mess didn't mean I could ignore a rare opportunity to witness Trinity's triumphant return to Golden Dunes. No way I'm missing that.

FOR AS THOUGHTFUL and egoless as Trinity typically is, we both knew tonight was about her. While the makeup was doable on her own, she still needed some physical assistance doing her hair and some *opinion* assistance with her outfit. And tonight, she was looking to *shine*.

"These for sure..." she said under her breath, digging through the closet. "Oh, and this... and I *have* to wear this..."

Okay, well maybe she didn't need *much* help from me. Trinity was swift and efficient in her selections, settling on bright red, sparkly crop top, short jean shorts and white cowboy boots. The red white and blue made her look like a patriotic firecracker. The makeup was already done, but she led me into her bathroom to assist with her hair. Trinity opened the top drawer and pulled out a metal device.

"Ever curled hair before?" she asked, handing me the device. I stared at it, confused how a metal rod with no clips or anything could possibly curl it. Trinity clocked my confusion. "Evidently not..."

She spent the next 15 minutes giving me a full tutorial on the ins and outs of a curling rod. Patient as always, she let me practice on her hair as I created curls at the pace of a tortoise. But Trinity's long, full, blonde hair was a dream to work with.

"This is why keeping healthy, strong hair is a *must*," she explained. As someone who'd recently adopted her hair care routine, I completely understood.

Despite making a few mistakes, Trinity's smile beamed the entire time as I transformed her straight hair into a beautiful bouquet of waves and curls. I think she thoroughly enjoyed both the result and the process of teaching her interested nephew.

"Gorgeous, gorgeous, Anderson!" Trinity cheered, stepping away from the mirror and admiring my work. "Are you sure you don't wanna quit nursing and just do hair for a living?"

I laughed as I helped with the final touches, clipping a big, sparkly red bow in the back. "Voila! My firecracker Aunt!"

Trinity hugged me the best she could, tearing up at the final transformation. Though it didn't take long for her to realize only half the job was done. "So what are *you* gonna wear?"

Not that I was dreading putting on another girls' outfit, but I certainly wasn't inspired to flash it up either, still feeling a little off and guilty from all the dressing of late. "Maybe just some jeans and a nice shirt?"

Trinity's giant smile vanished, clearly disappointed that I

wasn't equally psyched to get dolled up tonight. "Hmm, alright. Well, whatever you feel comfortable in!"

MY DECISION not to go all-out dressing up didn't hinder Trinity's enthusiasm for long. In fact, she raved almost the entire ride there about how much she missed being outside, seeing people, and, as she put it, being 'immersed in the holiday'.

It felt weird pulling up the Golden Dunes both A) *not* as an employee, and B) *with* Trinity. In a way, I was seeing how the other half lived. The employees were warm and kind to her. Many welcomed her back or asked if she could use extra assistance as her arm was still in a sling. To witness this attention from the perspective of a member felt strange. The ones who didn't recognize me simply treated me as if I *were* a member. The few who did gave me a bit of a double take, then smiled and moved on.

And *boy* did the members come out in full force for the holiday. Kids and adults alike donned their flashiest, Independence Day garb as they waltzed around the property. The clubhouse and surrounding grounds too were drowning in festive, patriotic decor. Flags and flag-themed decorations covered every inch of the place. I felt like I couldn't turn a corner without running into a cut-out of Uncle Sam, a bald eagle, or anything that wasn't red, white, or blue.

Past the clubhouse in the back, the formerly calm main lawn had undergone a complete transformation. To our left, a rock band played onstage. The opposite side featured a giant party tent, home to multiple serving stations and dozens of dining tables, each with their own patriotic flair. Members and their families lined up at the stations, eager to take part in the GDCC pig roast tradition.

The energy was electric and nobody seemed to be enjoying themselves more than Trinity. While she'd complained about the membership in the past, she certainly didn't show it today. In the course of an hour, I must have been introduced to thirty different people, all friendly acquaintances of Trinity's. None of them I recognized from the tennis courts, though I wondered if I *had*, would they even remember me, the lowly tennis attendant? Everyone was friendly, sure, but in a surface-level way. 'How are you?' and 'So good to see you!' being uttered less as a genuine inquiry, and more as a meaningless greeting meant to check a box.

Only for a brief moment did we run into Tara who, understandably, was *deep* in the weeds with work. Though she never asked me to help out today, I still felt a little bad 'switching teams', (for lack of a better term) and showing up as the guest of a member. Instead, I shoved all those dissonant thoughts aside, put on a gleeful face and followed Trinity's lead.

And so we carried on with a wonderful evening. The food was delicious, the vibes immaculate, and as the sun set, we watched the band perform high-energy bangers as everyone anxiously awaited it to get dark enough for fireworks. I was really starting to understand the appeal of GDCC membership.

I stepped away for a few moments to help myself to another slice of apple pie — or rather, 'patriotic pie', as the index card in front of it read. I must've been so in my own world that I didn't even notice who was standing behind the counter.

"*More* pie?" I heard someone say.

Fuck. I knew that voice. Of *course* it was Kelly.

I stammered nervously, though I'm not entirely sure *why*. I was merely fetching a second helping of an awesome desert. "Oh, uh, hi!" I said, awkwardly fixing my hair in front of him.

"Are you always this nervous around guys?" he asked, chuckling as he got back to work stacking plates. He was in a standard black button-down and pants, accented with the golden GDCC logo on his shirt pocket — the same thing every other employee was wearing today.

"I'm... It has nothing to do with *guys*, Kelly," I shot back, immediately on the defensive. "I'm just hanging out with Trinity tonight."

"I can see that. I almost didn't recognize you, not in your dress," he said. I held my hand out for him to quiet down, as if my dress-wearing was secret... which it *kinda* was, I guess.

"You know I don't always wear dresses," I told him sternly. "Like how *you're* apparently capable of putting on a damn shirt for once."

"Oooh, got me!" Kelly said sarcastically. "Well, I hate to say you'll be seeing me shirtless again in a couple days."

In a couple days? Why? Is he coming over again? I nearly asked him, but was interrupted by Trinity from behind.

"Kelly, hey!" she said brightly. "Gettin' some hours?"

He nodded. "Work's work," he answered, almost changing his demeanor completely around Trinity. He was no longer a sarcastic, teasing jerk. I guess you gotta put the charm on *some-*

times to get by in life. "I was just telling Anderson—" he began, but was swiftly interrupted by Trinity.

"About your work at our place? Yes. We'll see you then!" She answered, then grabbing my arm and ushering us both away. It was an odd end to the conversation, though I'll take *any* chance to get out of a conversation with Kelly, no matter how odd.

Even the social butterfly Trinity was getting a little petered out from conversation, so we decided to get an early seat for the fireworks. The first hole fairway on the golf course was the designated viewing spot, and each member was supplied a lawn chair for a comfortable view. A bit overwhelmed from the social interaction, I grabbed us a couple of seats and set them up far away from any other chairs.

"God, I can't have another bite," Trinity announced, rubbing her exposed belly and leaning back in the chair. "If I eat any more, I'm 100% bursting out of these shorts."

I laughed a little, half-listening as I stared into the quickly darkening sky. Trinity looked over at me. "You've been a little off tonight, haven't you? Shit... Did I introduce you to too many people?"

I shook my head. "No, that's not it. I'm just..." I paused, deciding how introspective I wanted to get with her.

Eh... maybe not much. "Just a little overwhelmed as of late," I told her.

Trinity took a sip from her drink. It was her fourth glass of wine by my count, but damn it if she didn't deserve to let loose a bit. Plus, I'm more than happy to be the designated driver. Safer for me to not drink too much meeting all these new people anyway.

She never ceased to impress me, this woman. Her extreme confidence was legitimately inspiring. She wants to put on a fun outfit? She does it. She wants to say 'screw it' and talk to a bunch of people at the club, despite feeling self-conscious about her bruises? She fucking goes for that too.

"How the *hell* did you do it?" I asked somewhat bluntly.

"Whatcha mean?" Trinity asked, rightly not understanding my vague question. "How'd I get a membership?"

I gestured to the clubhouse. "Not just the membership. Everything. You build a freaking incredible life, you know that?"

Trinity coolly nodded. "I'm lucky, Anderson. I should probably remind myself more of that." Trinity turned to me. "Lucky to have *you* this summer, too. You've been a godsend."

Her words were kind, but I shook my head because I wasn't fishing for praise.

"No, I've only been here a blip. But this whole life you built... Can I ask... *Why'd* you choose to do it alone?"

There was a wavering look in her eyes. "I mean... that's not entirely the case." She looked over at my bewildered face. "Have we never really talked about this? About my ex?"

So there *was* an ex. "No, you never told me."

She huffed. Clearly, this wasn't a subject she loved, but something about the moment was helping her open up. Or maybe just the alcohol.

"Well, there's not much to tell. I was with this man, Vince, for almost eight years — before Old Buffalo, by the way. Back when I lived in LA. And yeah, Vince and I were both go-getter entrepreneurial types, fresh out of college. We loved each other and motivated each other to go after what we wanted... It was pretty fucking great."

"So what happened?"

Trinity just shrugged. "Things just... didn't work out. The short answer is he pinned some problems on me that weren't my fault, I probably overreacted to a lot of it... You know, relationship drama shit." Trinity stared up into the sky. "So here we are."

It was obvious there was more to the story, but getting Trinity to open up even this much I should consider a win. "I'm sorry it didn't work out."

"Eh, it's fine. In the past, you know? I never really saw myself as a relationship person anyway. Even before Vince. But he had his good qualities and, you know, dating anyone is a leap of faith. But leaps of faith are what get you ahead in life."

Leave it to Trinity to so casually drop such profound thoughts.

"Do you still see guys?" I asked nervously. It was something I genuinely wanted to know, considering I'd never seen one come around the house.

"Relationships are kinda spoiled for me..." She turned to me and smirked a little bit. "Every once in a while I'll succumb to an urge though. I mean... who doesn't?"

I gulped, a little afraid to discuss this kind of topic with my Aunt. "Hmm," was all I said.

"I barely dated in high school. Even less in college." She laughed to herself, remembering something. "For what it's worth I even kissed a few *girls* in my youth."

"Really?" I answered, honestly a little surprised.

Trinity nodded. "Oh sure. Haven't in a long time. But hey, I never wanna rule it out in the future."

I sat there, not sure how to respond. As the non-romantic type, I didn't really have much to contribute.

But Trinity kept going on. "Have *you* kissed any girls?"

Fuck... despite developing a relatively open relationship with Trinity, we never really talked love and relationships. It just wasn't our thing. I guess I couldn't avoid it forever.

"A few," I answered. "Not in a long time though. I haven't really focused on it."

But now, Trinity was getting a little more serious. I looked around at the people filling their seats on the fairway, hoping they'd start this fireworks show soon.

Trinity took another sip of her wine. "Have you ever kissed a *guy*?"

I blushed, feeling extremely embarrassed for some reason. "Uh, no," I squeaked out.

"Would you?"

Fuck, could these fireworks just start already? "I mean..."

Trinity cut me off. "I'm sorry, you don't have to answer that. There's pros to each. Girls tend to be softer and gentler, which is nice. But kissing a guy? Especially a bigger, *handsome* guy who's like, *really* into you? Ooh! Anderson, there's nothing like it."

I chuckled as she sat there hormonally fan-girling over the way guys kiss. "Heh, maybe I'll have to try it someday."

She whipped her head to me. "Really? You would?"

While I'd answered half-heartedly, she seemed extremely amped. But this was only a hypothetical, so my answer — even if there was a *seed* of truth — didn't really matter. "I mean, yeah. Like maybe *someday*."

Trinity let out a huge sigh and slumped back into her lawn chair. "Ah, oh my god that makes me feel so much better."

She was acting weird again.

"Why would that make you feel better?" I prodded.

The sky was fully dark by now, and down deeper on the golf course I saw movement from the fireworks operators. The show was about to start.

"Okay, so *please* don't be mad at me, but you know how Kelly's coming over in a couple days?"

"Yeah..."

"He's not coming to do any yard work," Trinity said bluntly. "He's coming over to play your pretend boyfriend in a Princess Trinity video."

BOOM!

I heard the first firework explode just as she finished her sentence. Or maybe it was the bomb she just dropped on me.

12

Did Trinity personally know the firework technician? Or maybe have some sort of inside info on when *exactly* the show would start? Because she couldn't have picked a better time – for *her* – to have dropped this news.

There I sat, fuming but silent, waiting for the explosive, patriotic beauty happening above our heads to end. I was doubly pissed at my aunt. For one, she had gone ahead and brought in a guy to be my boyfriend on camera — a risky, unsettling proposition to begin with. But even if I were down for that, she simply couldn't have picked a worse guy to do it with. *Kelly? Seriously?* Of all men in the world, why did she have to pick the most annoying one on the planet — and one I found myself constantly embarrassing myself in front of? Trinity was lucky I'm not a huge fan of fireworks to begin with, because I'd be triply pissed if she ruined the show for me.

The sky lit up in chaotic, red, white, and blue glory as the final fireworks popped and sizzled, returning the country club to darkness and garnering applause from everyone present. Everyone except *me*.

Trinity looked over sheepishly. "Problem?"

"*Yes*, there's a problem! In fact, a million problems!" I started blowing up, but noticed other members walking nearby.

"How about we discuss in the car," Trinity said calmly, motioning for me to pick up our lawn chairs.

It was a long, uncomfortable walk back to my Kia in the parking lot. I was physically wiped from all the socializing and stress of the evening. Trinity was even a little burnt out too, offering friendly but distant waves to some of the folks we talked with throughout the night.

"You know he hates me," I said coldly, buckling up in my seat. "You've seen how he acts around me, haven't you?"

Trinity shut the door and buckled up too. "Kelly's not a bad guy. Maybe he's not always super chipper and friendly, but I trust him and he does good work. Plus, he agreed to do this so he can't hate you *that* much."

I mean... I *guess* that's a good point. Kelly knows exactly what he's getting into. Though it's entirely possible he thought it'd just be another opportunity to tease me for staring at him.

Trinity sighed as we made our way past the guard stand and back onto the main road. "Maybe this isn't my business to share... but you know how there's a couple types of people here in Old Buffalo?"

"Country clubbers, tourists, and..." I paused, not wanting to say it. "Poor people?"

She rolled her eyes, not caring for my terminology. "*Lower-*

income folks, but yes. Kelly's family is in that camp. The guy graduated high school and, as far as I can tell, *wants* to go to college. But
his parents who are… let's just say, a little difficult… aren't giving
him anything. So when I met him at the pool, I told him I'd give
him work whenever I can. Yard work, house chores, and…"

"…now he's posing as my boyfriend," I finished her thought.

"Mhmm," she nodded. "Well, *Andie's* boyfriend. Don't worry,
you don't have to date him." Trinity chuckled. I even laughed
just the tiniest bit.

"I got the idea from a new perfume brand called *Mystique*.
It's sexy, it's mysterious… I thought bringing in a 'mystery man'
for Andie would be fun for the viewers. I dunno, maybe I'm
over my skis on this."

"No, no, that's a cool idea," I told her, looking ahead at the
road. The lack of streetlights around here made driving require
most of my attention.

"Kelly doesn't want to show his face, which I understand.
But I was hoping that with how comfortable *you'd* been
getting… maybe you'd finally show yours?"

This all was coming together so fast. I knew that once I
show my face, I can't *un*show it. Still, like how Trinity was
'Princess Trinity', a character, I'm only playing 'Andie', another
character. In a roundabout way, I wouldn't really be showing
my true self at all. Maybe I could live with that…

"What'd you say earlier? Leaps of faith are what get you
ahead in life?" I asked. Out of the corner of my eye I saw Trinity
smile and nod. "Then consider this a leap of faith. I'll do it."

Trinity ecstatically clapped the best she could. "Oooh yay!

Anderson you're the best! Gah, I already have outfit and makeup and hair ideas… You're gonna look *great*…"

THAT CAR RIDE home turned out to be a pivotal point in my mindset toward dressing up and acting feminine. Even though I was playing the character of 'Andie', I'd be showing my face in all its glory, and confidently representing a girl on camera. Beside maybe a little makeup and editing filters, there was nothing for me to hide behind any longer.

So when the next day I showed up to work and saw Janice had booked me for another tennis lesson, without hesitation, I changed into my women's tennis outfit and confidently took to the court for an entire hour.

I wish I could say she'd grown leaps and bounds between our lessons, but Janice's skills were more or less the same. However, with one lesson already under our belts to become familiar, the conversation flowed much easier and it made for a genuinely pleasant, enjoyable hour.

"How's your Aunt, by the way?" Janice asked as our lesson concluded. "I hope this isn't intrusive, but I saw you and her from afar last night. She looked *stunning*."

I nodded, agreeing. "Totally. It was kind of her re-emergence. I think if all goes well, she'll be getting out of that sling very soon and into physical therapy."

Janice smiled warmly. "I'm so happy for her. Tough start to the summer, but I'm glad things are looking up. And hey, being as beautiful as she is, she's got *plenty* of time for a little dating before cuffing season rolls around!"

I gave a courteous laugh as Janice handed me another $100 bill. "I talked to Tara, she said we can keep this between us."

My eyes popped. I still hadn't gotten used to the sight of such quick money. "Janice, you're *extremely* generous. Thank you."

She winked. "Just don't tell my husband. Tootles!"

I stared at the bill as she walked away from the courts. My leaps of faith were already literally paying off — *literally*! Though as nice as the money was, what stuck in my head was her funny comment about Trinity's dating life. I liked Janice, but certainly not to the point where I'd be comfortable sharing her lack of interest in it. And little did she know, the one who in a strange, twisted way was *closer* to having a boyfriend — albeit a *fake* one — was me.

The way the courts and attendant stand were set up, I didn't have a great view out onto the property. The chain link fence was obscured by a mostly opaque green material that acted almost like a two-way mirror. Easy to see in, hard to see out. So I could never tell if Kelly ever walked by.

The pool was so out of the way that it really wouldn't make sense. Unless of course he wanted to strut by the courts, flaunting his three sexy lifeguard friends and laughing at the long-haired boy teaching tennis in a skirt. Or more than likely he simply doesn't care.

Well, obviously *I* don't care either, but considering his willingness to pretend to be my boyfriend, you'd think he'd stop by at least once, right? Whether to jeer or just say hello? Maybe it was the confidence of just having been handed $100, but unlike after my previous lesson with Janice, I didn't change out of my skirt. I kept my high socks, my women's shirt, and my scrunchie securely in my cute, bouncy ponytail. If Kelly *does* walk by, I want him to know I'm not scared.

"I'M BETWEEN THESE FOUR..." Trinity said, pondering some tops laid out on the living room couch.

She was always a little overwhelmed and indecisive on shoot days, but honestly, today I would've appreciated less indecision and more empathy. After all, any amount of 'perfect outfit picking' couldn't offset the nerves from showing my face on camera as Andie for the first time.

Yes, I've *technically* done this before, but Lumber Lane, MooMoo's and the Golden Dunes tennis courts were each a *maximum* of a few dozen people. Today, I'm putting on my best feminine face for tens of thousands.

"How the hell do you showcase a perfume anyway?" I asked, standing there in just a bra and panties, waiting for my aunt to pick something. "You can't smell through a screen."

"Well *duh*. That's why outfit selection is even *more* important. You need to pair the scent of the fragrance perfectly with the energy of the outfit. Everything must be in harmony."

I made sure to wait for her to look away before rolling my eyes. I think she got the hint, because moments later she made her final pick.

"This, this, and these," Trinity declared, referring to a tight, black leather skirt, a black long-sleeve sweater, and black Chelsea boots.

"So you want me to look dangerous?" I asked.

Trinity groaned. "Not *dangerous*. Edgy! *Mystique* is dark, mysterious... An all black look will suit you nicely."

She gestured for me to put on the clothes. It wouldn't be *my* first choice, but certainly beats standing here in a bra and panties any longer.

With the full outfit on, Trinity took me into her bathroom to get my hair and makeup done. I was far too early in my makeup journey to have any opinions in this department, so I deferred completely to my aunt. What we settled on was a heavy eye makeup look — complete with heavy mascara, dark eye shadow, and thick eyeliner. She heavily contoured my cheeks to accentuate my feminine angles. Then, the pièce de résistance: bold, sparkly red lips, achieved first with careful lining, filled in with a deep red lipstick, and coated in shimmery, sultry gloss.

"Va va voom, girlie!" Trinity cheered her own work. "I've still got it! And even better, we used three gifted products to add into the review!"

I took a moment to admire my stunningly beautiful makeup, but knew I wasn't out of the woods until my hair was complete. Though Trinity quickly made it clear *her* job was done.

"Nuh-uh!" She put her hand on my shoulder, reached into the cabinet, and pulled out the hair curler. "*Your* turn."

Damn it. I guess I can't expect a free ride *every* time.

It took around 20 minutes, but with careful watch from Trinity, I was able to turn my straight, boring brunette hair into something much more fun, flirty, and feminine. The long waves bounced around my shoulders as I shook my head back and forth.

"Ah-ah, careful there!" Trinity reminded me. "Your hair will catch in your makeup! Ladies must be daintier when their hair and makeup are done."

For the final reveal, Trinity led me back into her bedroom for a look in the full-length mirror. Simply put, I looked 100% female. Actually, no. I looked *1000%* female. Literally every inch of my body screamed 'bold, confident, sexy *woman*'.

My alluring, brunette waves and bold, dark makeup with a red lip drew the eyes in. The tight black sweater was slimming on my body and helped sell the illusion of my two little, perky breasts thanks to the padded bra. My leather skirt was short and daring, leaving little about my smooth, slender legs to the imagination. And the heeled Chelsea boots gave that small but necessary height boost to make my lower half as captivating as possible.

Through and through, I was one fucking *hot* 20-year old woman.

"Jesus... *Well done...*" I complimented, practically speechless. I turned around and caught Trinity staring behind me, shedding a tear. "Are you–"

"I'm okay, I'm okay!" she quickly wiped away the tear, embarrassed. "I'm fine. Seriously, Andie, you look *magnificent*."

What else could I say? The credit belongs to her.

Moments later, we heard a faint knock from the front door.

"Just in time," Trinity said. "Wanna go get your man?"

I groaned at the prospect of such a wonderful moment being ruined by Kelly's negative presence. But this was our deal.

"*Pretend* man," I reminded her.

"Wait! One more thing!" Trinity rushed into the bathroom and returned with the tiny bottle of *Mystique*. She put one spritzed on my neck and one on each of my wrists. "*Now* go get him."

I thought it best to exit the room before Kelly gets irritable waiting at the door too long. By now, I had enough practice walking in heeled boots that I wouldn't foolishly stumble up to him. One deep, soothing breath and I opened the door.

"Hey," I said. "We're waiting for you."

"I've been waiting here too," he answered quickly.

Kelly was dressed in an equally semi-formal look. Light gray dress pants with a black button-down shirt tucked in and held up with a black leather belt. He had three buttons undone on the button-down, revealing a metal chain necklace.

I felt nervous standing there in the hall with him, alone. At least with my heeled boots, his 6'5" frame towered over me just a *little* less. But jeez, was Trinity *intentionally* taking her time?

"Three buttons is a little much, no?" I asked. "And is the chain new? I don't think Trinity's gonna want you in that. It's too casual."

Kelly shot me his little dry smirk. "You get snippy when you're nervous, don't you?"

I felt myself turning red, though my makeup probably hid it. "*I'm* not nervous! *You're* nervous!"

He raised an eyebrow and laughed a little. "Well, I know *you* insulted *my* outfit, but I'm gonna be the bigger man and say you look nice. Your perfume is... pretty."

Hmm. This being his first compliment, I didn't entirely believe its sincerity. But I knew I couldn't just retort with another dig. "Thanks," was all I said.

Finally Trinity broke our silence and greeted Kelly with a big hug. "Ah, you look so good! *Exactly* what I had in mind."

Kelly smugly turned toward me. "Glad *someone* thinks so."

I groaned at his rude comment but Trinity laughed it off. "You two are so cute. Fighting like a little couple."

Both of us whipped our heads to Trinity and she quickly backed down. "Alright, alright, sorry! Let's get to it."

Because I was revealing my face for the first time, the first video Trinity wanted was a solo shot of me waving into the camera, then leaping back and doing a dance to some pop song. She also had me strutting down the house stairs, staring out the window, and smizing into the camera and spraying the perfume.

A *lot* of the things I did on camera felt silly. But this was the genius of Trinity. *I* was the one in my 20s, yet *she* had complete knowledge of sound trends, popular songs and dances, and the ability to caption and narrate videos to maximize both enjoyment and algorithm success. I've long since given up trying to argue against her proposals.

For the next series of videos we brought in Kelly — though notably only from the neck down. For *this* I was actually thankful he was so tall because we could easily have my whole body in frame while keeping his head out of sight. He clearly put effort into styling up his hair a little bit and maintaining his stubble, even if it was just for Trinity and my sake. That's *one* good thing about him.

The second round was mostly the same – dances, poses, holding up products. Gratefully she didn't have me touch him too much beyond holding hands and walking up and down the hallway. But some of those physical contact ones proved to be the trickiest.

"Can we redo that one?" Trinity asked during our hand-holding. This was the fourth time she'd stopped us. "Andie you've got a weird look on your face."

Kelly looked down at me. "Yeah, I see it now."

"See *what*?" I snapped at him.

"You're just so nervous," Kelly answered dryly. "I can't help it if it's funny."

I snarled again. "Jesus, I'm *not* nervous!" Realizing I was still holding his hand, I yanked it away.

"Alright, let's everybody cool off," Trinity said. "Passion's good, but not if it's *too* heated. Anyways, I think we got it."

Trinity had such an efficient, scripted plan and *Kelly* was making everything harder. I understand that he needs the money, but how she considers him a hard worker is beyond me.

"No. Let's do one more." I insisted. "I'll be better."

See? I can be the bigger person too.

Another two more takes and we had the perfect hand-holding spin into a cute smile at the end. Watching back the take on her iPhone, it was clear I'd nailed it.

"Damn..." Trinity muttered. "I know we can't see Kelly's face... but you two have some *serious* chemistry."

"Thank you," I said proudly, looking to take full credit. I looked to Kelly who was surprisingly giving me a golf clap.

Trinity glanced down at the footage one last time, then looked over to the open couch. Then back at me. "I think we're pretty set for today... But I was wondering if we could try *one* last thing."

Kelly nodded. "Sure, anything."

Looking to match his helpfulness, I took a step forward too. "Anything."

Trinity made a weird expression. "Well... hear me out. Kelly, do you mind taking your shirt off?"

"When *doesn't* he?" I said under my breath.

He shot me glare. "Sure," he answered.

Trinity stepped toward the nice, decorative living room couch and gave it a feel. Then, she closed the curtains on one side of the room. Then, the curtains over another window. The room wasn't pitch black, but it was sufficiently darker. "Lie down please, Kelly."

Kelly was a little perplexed. Frankly so was I. But he none-theless unbuttoned his shirt and did as told. Trinity grabbed the tripod and positioned it in ten or so feet from Kelly.

"What is this, reverse *Titanic*?" I pointed out, considering how Winslet-esque this was shaping up to be.

"Well, you're part of this too," Trinity said, focusing the shot. "Yeah, this'll work."

Now I was starting to get a little nervous. "What kind of shot are you thinking?"

"Obviously if this is out of either of your comfort zones, let me know... But you said you're down for anything," Trinity reminded us. Though she even looked a little unsure herself. "I noticed we haven't really featured those pretty red lips yet. So Andie, I want you to get on top of Kelly, lean your head down, and plant a single sweet, little kiss on his chest for the camera. Okay?"

13

I paused for a moment, admittedly shocked by the request.

"You want me to... *kiss* him?" I repeated. "*Kelly.*"

The request was so sudden — and frankly, so *specific* — that I felt utterly thrown off. I mean, *what?* I had to look over to Kelly to make sure he heard the same thing. But to my complete surprise, Kelly didn't really miss a beat.

"I'm okay if you try," he said to me, not showing much emotion. "Just a kiss, right?"

"Yeah, but *you're* not the one kissing!" I shouted.

Trinity stood up, recognizing she made a mistake. "You're right, I'm sorry. Too much too soon, I get it."

Shit. I wasn't about to be the one who shuts down her idea again. I hated the thought that by me not being a team player, Kelly somehow won.

"Well hold on..." I held my hand out. "No, it's fine. I just... I'll do it."

Kelly was a little surprised by my immediate change of tune. Trinity too.

"Are you sure?" she asked.

I stood there, straightening my posture. "Yes. I'm a team player. I'll kiss his chest if you think it'll help."

"It's a sexy perfume," Trinity reminded me. "A sexy little photo or video could *only* help."

I was hoping that in return for my willingness to partake, Trinity would give me literally *any* guidance on how to do this without looking extremely awkward. But no. It was up to Kelly and I to figure this shit out.

Besides taking off my heels, I did no additional disrobing. Kelly, however, lied there with his shirt off, basically waiting for me to straddle him. *God* this felt so weird. But I bit the bullet and slid my hips and legs up onto his, and laid down to rest my head on his chest.

This was the closest I'd ever been to him — or hell, *any* man — without a shirt on. It all felt so... *intimate*. With my ear pressed against his chest, I could clearly hear and feel his heartbeat. The only thing separating my skin from his were my soft, brunette curls. My heart was racing, just as it'd been most of the day. Shockingly, so was Kelly's. His calm demeanor disrupted for the first time.

"Sorry, does it tickle?" I squeaked out.

"No, you're good," he replied, his voice wavering just a little bit. Oh, so he *was* kinda nervous. Interesting...

"Turn your head more to me," Trinity said, crouching and re-adjusting the tripod for a better shot. "Now give me a smize."

I shot her a smize and Trinity snapped a series of photos. The whole thing felt a little ridiculous, but with Trinity's editing skills I'm sure the end result would look as sexy as she intended. A tall, muscular man with his dainty girlfriend lying on him? At least on paper, this felt like a winner.

I shifted around a few more times and notably, each time I moved, Kelly's heartbeat jumped. I held back a laugh. Looks like close contact was superman's kryptonite. I knew it was unproductive and only served to slow us down, but I decided to mess with him *just* a little bit.

"Hold there for a second guys, I'm gonna get the perfume from my bedroom again. We need it in the shot!" Trinity scampered off leaving just the two of us alone.

"So I'm not the only one who's nervous," I noted, my head still gently pressed to his chest.

"What're you talking about? I'm fine." Yet his voice still wavered.

"You're such a liar! I can hear your heart beating," I picked up my head, repositioned my body so I was looking at him, face-to-face. "You're telling me I don't make you nervous?"

He swallowed sharply, but after a few seconds of silence he simply answered. "No."

"Even if I kiss you here?" I said, lifting my head and planting a gentle kiss right between his pecs.

Kelly gulped, but again, calmly told me, "Nope."

"Oh my *God* you two!" Trinity squealed, revealing herself from around the corner. "I freaking *pray* the camera was rolling." Kelly and I looked at each other, concerned that our little pretend-teasing-flirtation wasn't just captured.

"Ah! It was!" Trinity was over the moon. "See *this* is what I want. Something natural!"

Kelly quickly shot up from the couch, nearly launching me off of it. "We were just kidding around, Trinity. We don't have to use that."

Trinity was rewatching the footage, practically ignoring his pleas. "No need. This is perfect! Your head's out of frame the whole time..." With genuine pride, Trinity looked right at me. "*Damn*, Andie, I had no idea you had that in you..."

I was already back to blushing from embarrassment — not from what I did, but from Trinity *catching* me. "Just... ya know... playing around."

"Well it worked," she declared. "And honestly? I think we already have enough shots with *Mystique* featured. I say we end on a winner!"

Kelly sheepishly arose from the couch, a little stunned by how everything ended. I was too. Things between us got... *tense*. But for the first time it wasn't in an angry way. What was meant as teasing came across as something else. And it was received strangely well.

Trinity, always the good host, walked Kelly to the door after he put his shirt back on.

"I'll make my selections, edit everything, and send you a link once it's up," she told him, re-adjusting his collar for him.

"And you're not gonna tell anyone it's me, right?" he clarified. "No face and no name, okay? I don't like being the center of attention."

She pantomimed zipping up her lips, locking, and tossing away a key.

Kelly nodded to Trinity, made one last glance over to me but without a nod or even a smile, and went out the front door. Once it shut, Trinity moseyed over to me, still standing in my full outfit, hair, and makeup.

"*Quite* convincing, Andie..." was all she said on the matter. "Now help me clean this all up."

I TRIED my best not to think about my shoot with Kelly over the next couple days, and it was probably best I didn't, considering the packed work schedule I had coming up at the club.

To date, I'd only been given easy shifts where I handled simple reservations and rentals, and the folks caused very few issues. But this weekend was the long-awaited GDCC Tennis Championship.

Before I sell it *too* well, it's open-invitation and any member or child of a family member is allowed to enter. The Championship is split into four simultaneous mini-tournaments: Men's Elite, Men's Open, Women's Elite, and Women's Open. Essentially, if you think you're good, you go Elite. If you're there for fun, enter the Open. Based on the number of people who normally use the courts, I expected low attendance. But *boy* was I wrong.

In the week or so leading up to the big Saturday, our phones would ring constantly with reservations and it felt like every couple minutes the attendant stand desktop would ding with the alert of another sign-up. Everything pointed to this tournament being hectic and, if not properly executed, a complete and utter mess.

Tara had me arrive at the courts around 6:30 A.M. Saturday morning. *Nobody's* ideal start time for anything, but I suppose it's part of the job. In the world of GDCC Tennis, this was our Super Bowl.

In the spirit of 'all hands on deck', every part-time attendant was working today: that one boy Nathan, the Velmahos twins, and even the 40-something private instructor Greg was helping out — I guess looking for a little extra weekend cash.

"Nice to see you all so early!" Tara said with a forced cheerfulness. Clearly even *she* wasn't thrilled to be working before seven on a Saturday. "Nathan, Velmahoses, Greg... all of you've worked this tournament before. But this is Anderson's first time so let's give him the floater role."

Nathan, clearly a country club brat, audibly groaned at not getting what must be the 'easy assignment'. Helena and Lambros Velmahos seemed to accept their fate without issue, as did Greg. Even though I barely knew any of 'em, I already could tell they were preferable to Nathan.

Essentially, each employee was assigned one court and one tournament to run. Greg got Men's Elite, Nathan Men's Open, and the Velmahoses took the women's tournaments. Tara would run the attendant stand and handle registration snafus while overseeing the whole production.

My job was to 'float'.

Yep... Walk around, all day, and if anyone needed *anything*, I'd be the one making the runs to and from the courts.

Normally that'd sound wonderful, but on a day that's supposed to reach 90 degrees, getting the one job that *wasn't* in the shade sounded like a raw deal.

As the players started showing up, Tara gave us a final rundown and game schedule. As long as everyone followed her lead, it should be smooth sailing. Tara dispersed the others to their respective courts and wished everyone luck. But she held me back for a moment.

"Anderson, come here for a sec..." she said, holding up her hand to a member patiently waiting in line. "I just wanna say, I saw your post on Princess Trinity. Can I say you look absolutely *electric*?"

I'd been so occupied with work and studying that I hadn't even noticed Trinity posted yet. I guess my face was officially out for the world to see.

"Thank you," I replied. "It was... Well, it all came together."

"I'm pulling my hair out wondering who that mystery man is though... Eh, never mind, sorry. I'm overstepping!" It was actually kind of cute how Tara had trouble balancing her enthusiasm with professionalism. "What I meant to say was, since you seem to be openly wearing feminine clothing — and looking *killer* — I brought you an outfit you may wish to wear for the day instead. There was an extra in storage."

From beneath the counter, Tara pulled out what looked like, well, *not* a skirt, but a dress. A white, GDCC branded tennis dress.

I held it up in front of my body. The material was sturdy but lightweight and the texture extremely soft. Whatever the dress was made of felt like an absolute dream. Coupled with the dress were a pair of brand new white women's athletic sneakers, high socks, and an adorable black athletic headband with GDCC printed across the front in the signature gold lettering. The whole ensemble looked magnificent, but the guilt started setting in.

"I... I can't accept this. Isn't it unfair to have two uniforms when everyone else has one?"

"Pfft, please! Who cares?" Tara dismissed. "The *others* won't pull it off as well as you do. You deserve this."

I mean, I'm not one to turn down free things...

"Okay then," I said with a smile. "I'll change!"

Wishing to not fall behind, I speedily changed into my new uniform. Not only was it *way* cuter than my other look, but far more comfortable as well. And considering I'd be on my feet in the sun most of the day, this outfit was perfect.

My first instinct after stepping out was to worry about what others would say. Would people think I'm a freak for wearing a dress in public as a boy? What would the ramifications be? But I set aside those worries knowing A) Tara *gave* this to me, B) I already showed my face in a dress online and C) I knew I looked *damn* good. It's hard to beat the confidence of looking cute.

The four tournaments got up and running with little issue. I *did* get a few questionable looks from some folks as well as a particularly snide comment from Nathan, but beyond that, most people either didn't care or hid their judgment. Runs back and forth to the clubhouse for food, drinks, athletic tape, towels, and a million other requests kept me so busy that I barely got to watch any of the games. Even so, the ability to walk around the club feeling confident, free, unobstructed, and well, *myself*, was genuinely euphoric.

Each time I passed by the clubhouse, I had a slight fear of an awkward run-in with Kelly, though it appeared he wasn't working today. Maybe it's for the best. My mind was still twisting and turning, trying to figure out how to feel about the shoot.

As players got bounced, the courts grew less hectic. Some of the eliminated players stuck around and watched from the limited benches, but most left for other areas of the club or went home entirely. And after hours of constant requests, I finally found time to sit down. Each court was hosting its 'finals' match, though of the four, 90% of the energy and attention was focused on the Men's Elite court.

I walked up next to Greg who was overseeing the match.

"Everything go well today?" I asked.

Greg let out a big sigh, understandably exhausted. "*Long* day. But at least I get to watch a good matchup."

By the looks of it, he wasn't kidding. The match being played was *easily* the most intense of the tournament. On one side was a man who looked to be in his mid-30s. Balding, but everything else about him suggested he was youthful and in shape. According to Greg, he was a former college player at the University of Michigan, and a 'semi-local' who split his time between Old Buffalo and the Detroit suburbs. One hell of a player.

The player on the other side was quite the opposite. A polished, put-together guy with hair so platinum white he looked nearly albino. His height reminded me of Kelly, but this guy was *rail* thin and lacked the muscle mass of a swimmer. In fact, being *so* thin, he even looked a bit silly slinking around the court.

But it certainly wasn't affecting his play because this guy hit the ball *hard*. While probably less skilled than his opponent, his brute force was overwhelming.

"That's Bryce," Greg told me. "His Dad's a member and he just graduated from boarding school in New Jersey. Spends part of his summers here."

"He just gradua– *Wait*, he's only *eighteen*?" I asked, shocked at how young he was.

Greg nodded. "I used to give him lessons as a kid, actually. Funny thing is, he doesn't really *play* tennis. He's got a fencing scholarship to Michigan State. Not that he *needs* it though. His pop's loaded."

"Heh, I mean who *isn't* at this club," I replied, half-listening to Greg, half mesmerized by the boy's play. People who play *one* sport well is already impressive. But *two*? And at such a high level? It's quite the achievement.

"He's really something," I said in awe watching Bryce dart around the court, slamming the ball to finish off a point. It was a pleasure watching him play.

If anyone *looked* like a 'country club kid', it was Bryce. Knowing nothing of his personality, he appeared snooty and proper— even if his play style didn't exactly reflect it. But still, something about his scrappy, brutish play – maybe just the fact that he grunted *way* more than most guys do during tennis – captivated me. I'm a little embarrassed to say, but I even squealed a few times and broke into applause when he won a long, hard-fought point.

It didn't take long for Bryce to finish off the match, and Greg held up his arm in boxer-like fashion crowning him champion. It totally wasn't my place, but I felt a strong urge to go up and introduce myself. Maybe he could share a tip or something. But I thought it better just to hang back.

It didn't matter anyway, because Tara frantically called me over to the other courts to start cleaning up. "Have you been there the whole time??" she called out, peeved but not actually mad. "You're a floater, not a spectator!"

Meeting Bryce would have to be another time – if I even see him again at the courts at all. I started fast-walking over to Tara to get back to work, dress swishing behind me as my hips swayed, but something in me made me turn around one last time. And sure enough, Bryce was standing all alone in the middle of the court, staring right at me. Not a glance. What looked like a fully engaged, *interested* stare.

"Andie, come on!" Tara yelled again.

I gave him a smile and a little friendly wave. *Another time*, I thought to myself, and answered Tara's call. "Coming!"

OF COURSE TRINITY was thrilled that I publicly wore a tennis dress the entire day in front of over a hundred people. Honestly, so was I. It was a step toward discovering my true level of comfort. Another leap of faith paying off!

In fact, I was so motivated by a successful outing in a dress all day that I approached Trinity with a request she allegedly 'saw coming for weeks': I told her I wanted to wear girls' clothes more around the house.

And just like that, my wardrobe doubled. Andie time became less of a 'Princess Trinity thing' and more of an 'any given day thing'. Being constantly sent free clothes, makeup, and hair products, it felt like I would never run out of new things to try. Everything from tops and shorts to bras and panties would arrive, which we'd set aside 'for Andie', and I'd put them away in my drawers. While I still wore boy things more often than not, the ratio was *quickly* approaching 50-50.

All of this had some logic behind it, too. The views and follower counts for Princess Trinity were skyrocketing with the advent of an Andie face reveal and *particularly* the boyfriend tease. So much so that Trinity insisted Kelly come over for another shoot. A concept which I didn't necessarily *oppose*, but still had my doubts about.

I hadn't run into him at work once since our shoot over a week ago. He wasn't working the day of the tournament, and even on days I did work, he never once bothered to swing by. Maybe he really *does* hate me. Or did I finally just prove he gets nervous too, and doesn't want to show his face?

Nevertheless, it was a steaming hot Thursday afternoon when Kelly came over next. Trinity had the great idea to show-case Kelly's work in the garden in the next shoot and do a cute tea party scene. We were sent an adorable pink swing dress with a fun little strawberry pattern. It was vintage, it was girly... it was *perfect* for a tea party shoot.

Not often did I have reason to practice doing my hair and makeup, so in *that* regard, I absolutely looked forward to today.

I was using a flat iron for the first time that'd make my hair stick-straight and as long as possible. Styled into a middle part, I added a matching pink strawberry bow to the back of my hair. Of course, I painted my toenails and fingernails a sweet, light red to go with the strawberries on my dress. The ensemble was so cute on its own, I felt like I didn't even need much makeup. Just a bit of concealer, mascara, and a shiny, strawberry-flavored chapstick and I was good to go.

Downstairs, I heard Kelly arrive and Trinity answer the door. I couldn't hear everything, but wondered what Kelly's demeanor would be like today. Was he as 'game' as last time? Or maybe he showed up with a ton of new restrictions on what we could do — especially considering how popular the posts were.

"Ohh, fantastic!" I heard Trinity yell out from downstairs. "You know what? You're making me wanna change it all up. I actually have *just* the thing..."

Huh?

I didn't like them making plans without me, so I slipped on my white sandals and hustled downstairs.

"You're not starting without me, are you?" I said, stumbling in the room. Guess I came in a little too hot with these poorly-gripped sandals.

Trinity, of course, exploded upon seeing me. Kelly even looked impressed, though he didn't really say too much. Classic.

"Oh no! God... now you're making me second guess *again!* Andie you're such a perfect little doll!"

I hesitantly curtseyed to thank her, but insisted she explain.

"Kelly actually had the great idea that because it's nearly 100 degrees out, maybe we push the tea party shoot to another day."

Ugh! Are you serious? He's already trying to get out of it?

"Too chicken, I suppose?" I said teasingly, directed at him.

"No..." he answered. "I said maybe we should do something with the pool. I brought my trunks." Kelly held up his *non*-GDCC swim trunks – bright red with thin black vertical stripes.

Trinity snatched the trunks out of his hand. "And when he showed me them, it reminded me I have the *perfect* thing to match. I think I got it... God, *six* months ago?"

I didn't know what to expect, particularly from something Trinity kept shelved for six months. Maybe some frumpy, bathing suit dress or pool cover-up that she'd never wear in public? But it wasn't anything like that.

"It might take a little... *maneuvering*..." she began, reaching into a box that was in the living room and pulling something out. "But I think you can fit in this."

In her hands, Trinity held the daintiest, skimpiest little red micro bikini I've ever seen in my life.

14

"What the hell is *that*?" I immediately spat out. Of course I was shocked, but even *I* couldn't help but laugh. "That's not even clothing!"

"I know, it's tiny. But isn't it *adorable*?" Trinity lauded what *barely* classified as a garment.

Sure, the bikini *top* might look okay on me. It wasn't exactly padded, but loose enough that at the right angles, one might assume I have small breasts. But the bottoms were an entirely different story.

I took the bottoms from her hand and flipped 'em around. The back part was essentially a thong, covering up nearly nothing. Other than a small strip of fabric, my butt would be completely revealed. The front part wasn't much better. While I'd worn panties before — and comfortably, I might add — a big part of that was having room to maneuver and tuck my, uh, *downstairs business*.

But with *these*? I was given *maybe* a few square inches of area shaped into a sleek v-cut. The whole thing was to be tied together with a thin, red string.

"Trinity, be honest," I began. "Considering..." I gestured to my crotch, "...*this*. You think I'll fit?"

"Well, aren't you a little bit smaller down there?" she said, but quickly retracted it after remembering Kelly was present. *God,* this couldn't be more embarrassing. "Well, I guess you might want to shave, first."

Well now it's *really* awkward...

Not that I expected Trinity to know everything about me, but I hadn't exactly shared with her how... well... *into* shaving I'd gotten. My eyes must've told her all she needed to know though.

"You're... clean as a whistle down there?" she whispered. Though again, Kelly was *right there.*

I shot her a glare. "*Yes*. Okay?"

Trinity gave me an utterly useless 'got it' wink. "Just try it on, alright? It's too hot out to do the tea party shoot. You really want to sweat all that pretty makeup off?"

The combination of Kelly's chuckling and Trinity's insistence provided just enough pressure for me to reluctantly snatch the rest of the suit out of her hands and stomp upstairs to change... *again*. "You guys are lucky I'm so flexible!" I shouted from my room.

Well, the *good* news is the bikini technically fit me. The bad news is it was about as close of a call as possible. Some clever maneuvering created a somewhat-but-not-entirely flat illusion in the front. I felt naked — probably because I pretty much was

— but after twisting and posing in my mirror for a minute, I started understanding the appeal of this thing. Blessed with bigger hips than most boys, a bigger butt, and armed with plenty of practice posing as a girl, I actually looked quite good. Hair, makeup, and skimpy bikini... all together, I looked pretty damn hot. Maybe my good looks would shut Kelly up.

Kelly and Trinity were already out at the pool and when I did my dramatic reveal, Trinity's jaw dropped.

"Holy shit..." she muttered, hardly believing it was me. "I knew you'd look good... But I didn't think—"

"I'd look *this* much like a girl?" I completed her thought, doing a feminine little twirl to show 'em each angle. "Well, I guess I do."

"Yeah, you do..." Kelly added, notably without any of his sass or sarcasm. Mission accomplished, I suppose.

Kelly had already changed into his swimsuit, and with the sun only getting higher and the day getting hotter, we set aside any discomfort or judgment of the other and turned on the 'fake couple charm'.

Much like the last shoot, we started with relatively innocuous tasks and posing: Both of us with our feet in the water; Kelly applying sun tan lotion to my back; me flashing my butt, Kelly standing behind me with his hands on my shoulders. A few videos, several pictures as a couple, some solo shots and close-ups... Trinity got a great variety, and each time she showed me a sample, I was continually impressed with how convincing everything looked.

Everything looked legit — a fact that was feeling less and less surprising. But what was truly unexpected was how well

Kelly and I were actually getting along. To be clear, neither of us necessarily *enjoyed* the couple-y things... but holding his hand wasn't the straight-up burden it was last time. When he touched my shoulders, he was gentler and more careful. The snide remarks — from *both* of us — were much less frequent. Maybe it was Trinity's motivation and supervision, or maybe we were just getting used to each other. Either way, the tension was *way* down.

"You two wanna hop in the pool?" She asked. "Feels like we're done on land."

Kelly looked at me with a smirk. "Comfortable getting your hair wet?"

"Hey, I'm no chicken," I said, smirking back and proceeding to cannonball into the pool.

"Wait! I wanted to—" Trinity called out. But it was too late. Kelly jumped in moments later, making an even bigger splash.

"I think I win," he said as I coughed on some water that got in my mouth.

Trinity was grimacing. "Well I *wanted* to do some shots with your hair dry..."

All three of us laughed. "Sorry, sorry," I apologized. "What do you wanna see?"

Moving toward the shallow end of the pool, Trinity had us splash each other, play around, and generally just act cute in the pool. Kelly, going rogue, even swam beneath me and lifted me out of the water, hurling me into the deep end. Normally, I'd hate being thrown around like a doll, but something about the situation, his strength, being in a pool in the hot summer... I actually kind of liked it. All in all, the pool shoot was probably the most fun we had as a duo.

"Almost done," Trinity said, peering over the side of the pool. "What's the depth there? Three feet? Andie, how do you feel about getting on Kelly's shoulders?"

Kelly glanced over at me. By now, that didn't seem like an absurd request. "Good by me," he said.

"Same," I answered, then turned to Kelly. "Just be careful, okay?"

Kelly dipped under the water and, from behind, I mounted his shoulders. Then suddenly, like a whale breaching, Kelly stood up and up into the air I rose. Because he was so tall, my entire body went *really* high up and completely out of the water. Not wanting to fall, I squeezed my thighs as I squealed with concern.

"Don't drop me! Don't drop me!"

Kelly was *really* enjoying my fear and took full advantage. He strutted around the water, wavering side-to-side like a drunk walking on the sidewalk. But for safety's sake, he held my legs tighter. I had no idea why, but the tighter he held me, the tighter I grabbed him, even to the point that I folded my body over his head and held my head closer to his. Riding on Kelly's shoulders felt like riding a mechanical bull at one of those bars.

"You're gonna fall! You're gonna fall!" he laughed, spinning me around as I held on for dear life.

"Ahhh!" I kept squealing, much to the enjoyment of Trinity who was filming the whole thing. Maybe it wasn't the cute, romantic-looking shoot she was going for, but she wasn't stopping us either.

Eventually, Kelly was able to fling me off and my small but mighty frame collapsed into the water behind him. Needing a little bit of relief, I stayed under water a bit longer than needed. From my angle, I could see only Kelly's legs, facing me.

I'm not sure why, but something about those legs, those shoulders... *his strength*... was alluring. Getting flung around is always fun, but this felt different. It was peaceful and quiet under the water, and only after escaping the crazy ride on top of Kelly did I notice something. Something about a strong man being playful with me was... I don't know... *attractive*? And there was no better indication than the stirring I felt down below. Being flung around by a man was undoubtedly getting me a bit... excited.

Of course, I snapped back to reality when I reminded myself this was *Kelly* we're talking about — the guy who I simply couldn't avoid looking like a fool in front of and always getting teased for it. With my breath running out I returned to the surface.

"Alright, alright, that was fun but I think we should—" I began as I wiped the water out of my eyes. But I cut myself off when I saw Kelly staring at me. Not in a judgmental way, but in a 'what the hell just happened?' way.

"Uh, Andie..." he started awkwardly, then swallowed. I was about to ask him why he looked so off, but slowly, he showed me something in his hand. In his hand, right in front of me, were my bikini bottoms. I was bare, and on full display beneath the water was my smooth, bare package. And for once, the small size of my penis *wasn't* the concern. Because of my little bout of excitement, my 'little Anderson' was visibly and undeniably aroused.

SHIT!

"Ah!" I shouted. "Gimme those!"

I was full-on freaking out as I snatched the bottoms from him and yelled at him to turn around. He wasn't laughing, I wasn't laughing... even Trinity looked embarrassed for me.

I whipped around in the water and rushed to slip my bottoms back on and reposition my penis in the v-cut cloth, though with it harder than normal, proved to be an impossible task.

"I'm... I'm so sorry," Kelly said as I frantically maneuvered myself with my back to him. "I... I should go."

"Jesus... Fucking... Christ..." I wailed, not looking at him and putting full focus toward getting my thong back on and tying up the string.

He swiftly exited the water as Trinity tried to calm him down. Kelly seemed *legitimately* rattled.

"You got everything you want, right?" he said, drying himself off and not waiting for a real answer. "Good? I'll go then."

"Kelly, you don't have to leave so soon," Trinity insisted. "It was a mistake. Those bottoms were bound to fall off at some point."

God, WHY was she making things worse??

"I shouldn't have whipped you around like that," he said. "I'm sorry, Andie. That was really, *really* fucking dumb."

I stood there in the pool, frozen with embarrassment. Kelly had objectively seen my penis, and because of that, a fun moment quickly soured into one of the most awkward moments of my life.

It didn't take long for him to dry off and put his shirt and flip-flops back on. "My clothes are inside," he said, still extremely frazzled. "I'll grab 'em and get out of your hair. *Fuck...*"

Trinity's attempts to stop him were futile. The guy was spooked and he wanted out. He turned around one last time before going inside. "I'll, uh, see you guys around." And with that, Kelly shut the door and was out of sight.

The two of us stood silently. Me in the pool, Trinity on the deck. The sun beat down as the sloshing water slowed, adding to the painfully still backyard scene.

THE STING of my pool shoot gone-wrong slowly wore off throughout the rest of the day — though it wasn't easy. Trinity tried to talk to me about it, but nothing about my inadvertent flashing felt fun to discuss. Granted, she was far enough away that she couldn't tell I got *excited,* but the whole of it was humiliating nonetheless.

I locked myself in my room for most of the day. I joined Trinity for dinner but we stayed mostly silent. There was no mention of the shoot at all, and Kelly didn't come up once.

As the evening went on, I thought less about myself and more about him. My guilt was real. I wondered if I should reach out to him and text him to apologize — even if the situation *was* partially his fault. But objectively this isn't what he signed up for. Kelly had no expectation or interest in seeing what was beneath those bikini bottoms. I don't blame him at all for leaving.

Drifting off to sleep, I thanked my lucky stars I have practically no occasion to run into him at work. With how things were left, honestly, I'd be okay never seeing him again. If you thought I was avoiding the break room *before*? Now, I'd be treating it like nuclear fallout. Despite everything, I was able to fall asleep.

THE NEXT THING I KNEW, I was in a hazy, dreamlike state. Of course, *when* dreaming, you're never quite sure what's going on. Things are sporadic, unclear, and often make no sense. You're lucky to catch or even remember one detail. But this dream felt particularly lucid.

The setting was Trinity's living room, though Trinity herself was nowhere to be seen. It was late, so outside was dark but the room was dimly lit with warm, soft light. I was seated on the couch and upon looking down, noticed I was dressed in a blue tank top and short, black skirt — neither of which I'd never seen before. And I wasn't alone. From behind, I heard quiet footsteps.

Only now did I notice what was off about the room. The entire upper half of the room was covered in thick, hazy fog. The ceiling, fan, and anything higher than maybe five feet was completely cloaked in white mist. Including, as it turned out, a naked male figure that was now walking in front of me.

My dream-self gasped upon seeing the tall naked body. Of course, my first instinct was to shield my eyes, but the body strutted with a confidence like he didn't care who saw. I glanced upward but his head was completely obscured by the fog, visible only up to his shoulders. I sat there, still, as the man said nothing and didn't move a muscle. He didn't touch me either, and acted as if I wasn't even present.

At first I wondered if this body could be mine – a subconscious recreation of my embarrassing fiasco from earlier today. But this body was nothing like my own. Strong, tall, and trimmed but not clean-shaven. If anything, this body looked a lot more like Kelly's.

But clearly it *wasn't* him... right? If it were, wouldn't he say something? Why would Kelly be standing in front of me, naked and motionless?

Suddenly, the man made a move. Just one simple step forward, closer to me. Still not touching me, but close enough that, if I wanted to, I could reach him. And for a moment, I considered...

What? No! I shook my head furiously. Why the hell would I even *think* about such a thing? Kelly's body or not, the thought of doing anything with this figure was absurd.

And yet, my heart pumped faster. My eyes kept finding themselves drawn back to him. And the stirring down below that I experienced in the pool returned once more. Beneath my skirt, there was a sensation like nothing I'd ever experienced. A temptation that, admittedly, felt natural.

In a mad whirlwind of fears and desires, I managed to

convince myself that, for *just* one second, I could allow my lips to push forward, widen just the tiniest bit, and...

Suddenly, my head shot up from my pillow. In a cold sweat, I was awake, realizing I was still in my bed. There was no man, and there was no fog.

The room was silent. The house, dark. I leaned over to check my phone. 3:40 A.M. *Jesus...*

Everything I'd just witnessed was fake — merely my imagination. I spent the next five minutes taking deep breaths and reorienting myself. None of it – not the room, the man, or the near-contact I made with him – actually happened.

And yet, it all *felt* so real. The closeness, the bare skin, the innate urge to interact with him and explore that part of his body.

As I lied there in silence, trying to return to sleep, I realized and accepted two undeniable truths.

One, I just had a sexual dream about a guy.

And two, a not-so-small part of me wished it were real.

15

There are good nights of sleep and bad nights of sleep. Last night was both.

As exciting and revelatory as my dream and my subsequent self-admission were, there was no way in *hell* I could tell a soul about either thing. My sexual awakening had to remain a secret.

Trinity greeted me the following morning with a beautiful vegetarian breakfast spread she'd put together all on her own, complete with eggs, multi-grain avocado toast, and a few other delicious sides. We finally chatted about the day before, though as expected, she didn't notice my embarrassing excitement below the water. In fact, she claims she was far enough away that she didn't see anything at all. I guess that's *one* good thing to come out of it.

"I haven't reached out to Kelly yet, but he seemed pretty

frazzled yesterday," Trinity reminded me. "I think I'm gonna talk to him to make sure he's alright."

"That'd be nice, thanks..." I said, mostly agreeing with the plan. "Can I ask you something though? Kelly... is he, uh... is he straight?"

By Trinity's reaction, it wasn't the question she expected.

"Uh, as far as *I* know he is... Especially by the way some of those lifeguard girls talk about him."

"Hmm," was all I said at first. "I guess that tracks. Straight guys aren't hoping to catch a glimpse of a, uh... another penis."

"Andie, straight *girls* often don't wanna catch a glimpse of a penis," she chuckled as bits of egg spit out of her mouth. "Oof! Excuse me!"

Trinity's nonchalant attitude made me think that maybe, with the waving of the water, he didn't even notice I was aroused. Or that he even got a good view. Maybe I'd be lucky and get away with this embarrassing mistake scot-free.

THE TENNIS TOURNAMENT ended up being one of the more fun work days I'd had in a long time. Socializing with coworkers proved to be... well, *meh*. But it certainly could've been worse. The members weren't bad either. But it was being around fun, healthy competition that really made the day.

So returning to GDCC for a slow day of work stung just the tiniest bit. Not much interesting happened beyond me opting to wear the tennis dress again. I figured if I could get by without many negative comments in front of a hundred people, the dozen or so people I interact with today will be a breeze.

"Back at it with the dress!" Tara came up to me in a particularly peppy mood. "Love to see that, girlie!"

I didn't love that she called me 'girlie' — mostly because she was in her 50s and it felt a tad cringey. But I didn't object.

"It fits great, what can I say?"

Running into Tara at work was a usual occurrence, but the look on her face suggested something else was up.

"Well, I think that dress had a little bonus benefit, too. You caught someone's eye."

"Someone's eye? What do you m—" I began, but then it hit me. It couldn't be...

"Did you happen to watch the Men's Elite? There's this boy Bryce who was quite smitten with you."

Holy shit. *Bryce*? No way this is happening. My face immediately turned red. "Wha— well, uh, what did he say?"

"Well, uh, honestly not much... In fact, we didn't even *speak*. I received an email asking to pass along a message. He said he saw you at the tournament and thought you'd make a great date to the Golden Dunes Ball."

Ho. Ly. SHIT.

"What's the Golden Dunes Ball? Does Bryce think I'm a girl? Does he know Trinity?" I spastically drilled Tara with questions about literally everything she said, and she very kindly answered each. Essentially, the Golden Dunes Ball is a members-only gala held in the grand ballroom, and apparently members go *all out* for it, buying expensive outfits just for the occasion. The club hires a fancy jazz band, serves extravagant cocktails and food, and members get to hang out in lavish style, reflecting on the highlights of their summers.

As for thinking I'm a girl, I guess Tara cleared that up right away. Bryce, evidently, is actually aware that my name is Anderson and that I just happened to be wearing a dress that day. He just wants me to look pretty for the dance.

"So *none* of my, uh... *maleness* bothered him?" I asked.

Tara shrugged. "Guess not. Plus, who cares! You make a super pretty girl anyway."

"This is insane..." I muttered, soaking in the information dump. "I mean... genuinely, *legitimately* insane."

Tara giggled. "Obviously I didn't answer for you, but said I'd relay the message. After all, I, uh...

Tara paused, likely afraid to intrude with another personal question. "Well, I wasn't sure if you're even *into* guys."

I froze for a moment, suddenly faced with a question I didn't think I'd have to address so soon, if at all.

"Are you?" Tara asked after my silence.

"I... uh..." I stammered. Fuck, why was this so difficult to just say aloud?

"Yeah. I kinda am."

Her face lit up. "Oh my gosh, honey! That's fantastic! Do you think Bryce is cute?"

With the hard part out of the way, I felt much freer to geek out over Bryce who, yes, I absolutely thought was cute — even if a rail-thin body might not be my *exact* type.

Tara and I chatted about him for a few moments and mentioned that while she doesn't exactly know *Bryce*, she knows that his father is not only extremely rich, but well-respected in the Golden Dunes community. I guess he invests in businesses all over the country and his residence in Old Buffalo is just one of many.

"You know…" I said to her. "If the ball is three weeks away, I should probably get to know this guy first before accepting his invite. Not to mention the pressure of going to a members-only thing."

"So you wanna go on a *date* with him?" she asked.

It felt wholly bizarre that only a few days ago I wasn't even sure I was into guys, and now I was already setting up a date with one.

"I mean, we don't have to call it that, but… yeah."

"Eep! Lovely!" Tara squealed as she started walking back to the clubhouse. "I'll email him your phone number so you two lovebirds can set everything up!"

I couldn't believe it. Andie Saffron was going on a date. A date with a *boy*.

I SPENT the remainder of my shift cogitating over the crazy situation I'd just placed upon myself. A real part of me wanted to just take that blind leap of faith and see what it's like to date a boy. But of course, the unconventional method of asking stuck with me a little. Why email Tara, and not just come to the club? Plus, if he thought I was cute, wouldn't he have just approached me after the tournament? It seemed just the littlest bit strange. It's possible he's just a nervous guy. And I can *certainly* relate.

I'm probably looking at this too cynically. I should be flattered after all. Who in their first few days after accepting their attraction to men actually gets attention from one? How lucky am I?

Of course Trinity is gonna freak out when I share the news, so I spent much of my drive home wondering how I should even broach the subject with her. *'Hey, so not only am I officially into guys now, but I'm setting up a date with one'?* No... There had to be a more deft way to tell her without her losing her mind.

Pulling into the gravel driveway of her Lumber Lane home, I realized tonight *couldn't* be the night I tell her.

Why? Because *Kelly's* car was parked outside...

"Shit!" I literally said aloud to myself, putting my car in park and mentally preparing myself to see him inside. What the hell was he doing here? Did he come to embarrass me even more? I knew Trinity said she wanted to clear things up, but did it have to be in person?

"I'm home!" I called out, cautiously entering the house. Nobody answered, though through the living room and kitchen, I noticed the door to the backyard was left open.

Still, neither Trinity nor Kelly were in or around the pool. The water was calm and the late afternoon sun was beating down into the pool, unperturbed.

"Trinity? Kelly?" I called out again, this time getting a response.

"Back here!" Trinity shouted from what must be her garden. *Aha.*

"I haven't been back here in a minute! What're you g–" I began, but stopped abruptly when I noticed a wild addition.

Strung all throughout the garden, high and low, were cute

little fairy lights. The baby lights were scattered in bushes, nestled in flower beds, and hung high, zigzagging over the entire garden scene.

"Surprise!" Trinity shouted. "Kelly's been working on this all day."

"It looks... incredible..." I couldn't help but admit. Kelly stood there sheepishly, the look on his face indicating residual awkwardness between us – though not enough that either of us felt the need to run away.

"Thanks," he said, grabbing his neck uncomfortably. "And I kept my shirt on the whole time I did it."

I couldn't help but chuckle at our inside joke. "I'm so proud of you."

"They'll look even more incredible during our shoot!" Trinity announced, then put her arm on Kelly's shoulder. "He graciously agreed to do double duty."

Our *shoot*?

"Woah woah woah, I'm not even close to ready for that! I mean, look at me!" I said, gesturing to my tennis dress. I had no makeup on and my hair was held up in a messy, sweaty bun.

"That's okay. I've built in time for you to shower and gussy up." Trinity checked her phone for the time. "It's an hour or so until sunset anyway. We're doing a backyard style date at golden hour! It'll look gorgeous!!"

I'm not sure how Trinity did it, but she somehow talked Kelly into a third photoshoot despite the extremely embarrassing end to our previous one. And even if it still felt a little soon, there's no way I was declining now.

And so Kelly and I were herded back inside to get ready for

our 'date'. I, of course, went upstairs to my room and bathroom while Kelly used Trinity's. Sure enough, my outfit was already laid out on the bed so I could swiftly shower, clean up, and change.

The previous time I was given an *obscenely* feminine pink dress to wear, but now had Trinity had changed her mind in favor of something a bit more modest. Laid out on the bed was a simple, green cashmere sweater and a pair of light blue, high-waisted jeans. To dress up the look, however, she set out a pair of 3-inch ankle strap heels. The outfit, all in all, wasn't much to run home about. But *one* part of it certainly caught my eye.

You see, while Trinity often preselected my outfits – although less so lately – I couldn't think of a time she actually laid things out for me to wear. Which is why her underwear choice for me was so surprising.

I don't wear them all the time, but when I *do* wear a bra and panties, they are always of the simple and modest variety. After all, it's not like anybody would see them. But right next my outfit, *clearly* meant for me, was a baby-blue lacy bra and panties set. I held up the pieces, struggling to accept this is what she chose. The bra was soft, dainty, and delicate to the point a stiff breeze might break it apart. And the panties? My first ever thong, of course. Similar to the bikini bottoms I wore for our last shoot. I mean, *jeez*, wasn't she aware of the slip-up last time?

Still, the underwear was objectively beautiful and I genuinely couldn't wait to try them on and pose in the mirror. Though I couldn't help but wonder... Why for my date with *Kelly*? It just felt like an odd choice.

My clothing inspection came to an abrupt halt after Trinity

yelled from downstairs to complain she hadn't heard my shower start yet.

"Sorry! On it!" I answered, shuffling into the bathroom to turn myself into something presentable.

I WAS a little infuriated how all-out Trinity was going for tonight. Like I could already hear the sound of smooth, classical tunes coming from the speaker outside. The sun, still out, was fast approaching dusk – the objective, perfect time for softly-lit romantic photos.

I emerged from my room after a whole hour of getting my hair, makeup, and outfit pristine and presentable – though I might've been a *little* quicker if I didn't spend time posing and checking myself out in the mirror in my adorable new underwear. Even without my bra stuffed, I looked and felt shapely, sexy, and desirable – a fact that did wonders for my confidence.

Kelly was already in the garden when I got there. He too was dressed somewhat casually with a thin white sweater and jet black, slim-fit jeans with similarly colored boots.

"Hey," I said softly. "You look nice." As annoying as it was to play along with him sometimes, I decided to go for peace tonight, remembering how well things had gone at our pool shoot before it all fell apart. Somehow, the mocking and trading of barbs felt less warranted after accidentally flashing him.

"As do you," he said, looking at me head to toe, then taking a seat. "So we're taking pics?"

Hmm, a little cold... But I understand.

With music playing, drinks poured, and a quaint little table set up beneath the canopy of garden fairy lights, the scene was set. Aside from a few products we had to feature like a watch for Kelly and a selection of bracelets and rings for me, our only instructions were to be ourselves and sip away at the wine.

Being much less structured than our other shoots, I felt a hefty amount more pressure to be engaging and charming toward Kelly. Almost like... a *date*.

"Pretend I'm not here!" Trinity would remind us each time we broke conversation with an awkward pause to look at her or the camera, shuffling around the garden to get a million different angles. "You're doing great!"

So we did just that. Sat there, pretended we were alone, and just... *talked*. Small talk at first, chatting about people we knew at the club. Though Tara and Trinity were the only people we both knew *well*. Besides that, we stuck to GDCC, the town, and a few mentions of the local library that was briefly my home base for studying.

God, I'm just so bad in these situations... I reverted to my go-to of 'tell me a story about an arbitrary thing' – which only works if the other person is chatty and *interested* in that arbitrary thing. Luckily, I got him talking about his swimming career. As it turned out, Kelly was quite passionate about it. Hell, I even got a few smiles and shared laughs.

Dusk grew closer and Trinity graciously served us each a second glass of wine. Red for me, white for Kelly. As I only just learned, he had a bad experience drinking red wine in high school and has had a taste aversion ever since.

The more we chatted, the deeper we got in our conversation. Less about our immediate surroundings and our recent pasts, and more about our futures. I told him about the NCLEX exam I was preparing to take in the fall and how, once the season came around, I planned to move back to Chicago and find work at a big hospital. Somehow, he didn't mock me. He made no jokes. He simply replied, "I think that's incredible, Andie."

I clocked him calling me "Andie" without hesitation – like that's who I *am* to him now. He even shot me a little smile at the end.

Avoiding our no-go topics like the pool incident, the break room stare, this kiss on his chest, and any other past awkward interactions proved to be no trouble at all. Turns out, if you're forced into a situation where you *have* to talk to each other – and be civil in front of a relative taking photos and videos of you – it's not terribly hard. I genuinely couldn't believe it, but this 'date' with Kelly wasn't half bad.

Trinity had floated in and out, making runs to the house to get cleaner looks at the footage and pictures, but Kelly and I kept on talking, even when unprompted. One time we didn't even notice Trinity's absence of almost twenty minutes, noticing her return only once she placed a plate of crackers and fancy, sliced cheese for us to nibble on.

"Just since you're having so much fun," Trinity offered with a wink. "Cheese is the perfect, 'evening in the garden' snack, don't you think?"

I wasn't so sure about that claim, but saying so reminded me to glance up at the sky. Dusk was upon us, and the twinkling of the new garden lights all around us was simply enchanting.

"How are you so incredible?" I asked him, quickly adding on, "*At lights*! At installing *lights*."

He chuckled, but knew what I meant. "I have to admit, Trinity's not the only one I've worked for." He looked over to her. "She knows this."

Trinity nodded. "Kelly's done handiwork and installations for a bunch of GDCC members. And he always gets great reviews..." Then she noticed our empty glasses. "Can I get you some refills? I'll get you some refills."

With Trinity away for a moment, I felt comfortable enough for the first time to ask Kelly a burning question. "All these rich, Golden Dunes people... and the tourists... That's gotta be annoying, right?"

Kelly didn't react much, just chuckled a bit. "Feeling guilty?"

"What? No, I wasn't talking about me!" I said defensively, though recognizing the hypocrisy as we sat in my aunt's impressive backyard. "Well, point taken."

Kelly sighed and relaxed back in his seat. "I don't really think about 'em much. They're just kinda... here. My Dad *really* hates 'em."

He'd told me earlier about his strict, kinda-mean blue-collar father. A trait that we both shared – besides the *mean* part, I suppose. My father was nice enough, just distant and unengaged.

"For what it's worth, I definitely got a different reception on the 4th of July night as a guest than as a worker. Most people just ignore me at the courts."

Kelly nodded. "You're preaching to the choir. Your Aunt's a rare exception. A few others too. But 95% of those folks at the club, as far as I'm concerned, I wouldn't like talking to anyway."

For just a moment I considered asking him if he knew anything about Bryce or his father, but sensed this wasn't the time.

"But hey, I've learned to take care of myself and make money where I can. For a while, I thought I'd get shit from other employees that I was working on the side for the GDCC folks. Like I was a freaking simp for them, or something."

"What did they say?" I asked.

Kelly shrugged. "Some jabs here and there, but nothing bad. Gotta take risks for your own sake, right?"

"A leap of faith," I uttered, repeating Trinity's motto.

Kelly snapped his fingers. "Well said!" He took a long pause, quietly clearing his throat again. "At least to a certain extent."

His pause told me everything. He was referring to *this*. Our photoshoots. A straight guy being the secret boyfriend to a feminine boy functionally living as a girl. It was obvious this was one secret job he never wanted getting out.

"I only have white. Sorry, Andie." Trinity clomped in, revealing a bottle and breaking the silence. She handed me the bottle with the opener. "Lend me a hand?"

I opened the bottle and poured Kelly and I another glass.

By now, the sun was set and the sky – while not *totally* – was sufficiently dark. Trinity stood beside us, gears turning in her head.

"I know it's been a long shoot... But would you two mind *one* last set of photos? I like what we have, but I just wanna try one more look."

I nodded approvingly. Thankfully Kelly did too.

Trinity took a few steps back to give us some space, then sat on the stool she'd been using before.

"Okay, this one's gonna be a video. There'll be no sound, so what you say doesn't matter. And as always, Kelly, if I catch your face, it'll be cropped out later."

Kelly nodded, though he always got a little nervous when it came to framing.

"Great. Start by clinking glasses and smiling. Like you like each other."

We did as told. Both our smiles were small, but genuine. Almost like we *did* like each other.

"Now gaze into each other's eyes... for a little while. Get to know each other."

My thought was to be playful. But Kelly, without hesitation, gazed deep into my eyes. His intense, passionate stare nearly made me lose my breath. Jeez, where has *that* been...

"Grab his hand, Andie," Trinity instructed, which I did immediately. Kelly's palms were giant next to mine, and my delicate fingers paled in comparison to his. Have I never noticed this before?

"Can you give her hand a kiss?" Trinity asked Kelly, who hesitated for a moment. He nearly lost focus of my eyes, but held still, and gently lifted my hand to his lips where he softly kissed it.

Shit... I was starting to like this.

"Go sit on his lap," Trinity added, politely.

Almost in a trance, I rose from my seat and stepped over to Kelly, where he spread out his thigh to make room for me on his lap. Instinctively, I placed one arm around his back and with the other, I clutched his same hand that I'd held moments ago.

"Look at each other again," Trinity directed, moving a little bit closer with her camera but kept a healthy distance to serve the moment.

I looked deep into his eyes, realizing it'd been only twice that I'd been this close to him – once riding on his shoulders, nearly naked in the pool, and the other, placing my sweet, red-lipped lips on his bare chest as I straddled his body the night of our first shoot.

Then, with a suddenly disjointed mind, my dream from the other night crept back into my head. I was suddenly picturing the hung, naked figure that stood in front of me.

I was reimmersed in the dreamworld living room, back sitting on the couch in my little skirt, watching him. Wanting him. *Needing* to reach out and touch him. Salivating over the muscular body that was home to his impressive, tantalizing appendage.

Then suddenly the haze began to dissipate, merging my dreams and reality to reveal, *yes, Kelly's* body. His broad shoulders and tight abs right in front of me. His kind eyes looking down at me, inviting me to stand up and join him.

"Andie?" I heard Trinity call out from what sounded so far away. But I wasn't in her reality. I was in my own, thinking of Kelly and the things I wanted him to do to me.

"Andie!" I heard again.

I must've been spacing out, but I didn't care. Back in that dream, I was finally able to rise from the couch to meet my dream man. I wasted no time stepping up to him, grabbing his hand, and pulling him in for a deep, passionate kiss.

Then, everything went wrong. The dreamlike state disappeared. I was back in the garden, sitting on Kelly's lap. Trinity to my left, holding the camera in utter disbelief.

There I was. Kissing Kelly in real life.

16

Ever-so-slowly, with painful, stinging awkwardness, I pulled my lips back from Kelly's as I fully snapped back into reality. He was stunned. Trinity was stunned. *I* was stunned. I let a fantasy play out in my head, consume me, and manifest in real life.

"I'm... uh... I'm so..." I stuttered, wondering how I could even begin to apologize for kissing someone on the lips with zero warning.

For once, Trinity was speechless. Kelly, the man I'd been pretending was my boyfriend all night for the camera, motioned to Trinity to turn that same camera off.

I stumbled backwards as I stood up. He wasn't immediately mad at me. If anything, he seemed more disappointed in himself.

"I thought I could do this," he said. "I really did."

He looked beyond hurt. I needed to jump in. "Kelly, I didn't mean–"

But Kelly held his hand up, wanting to hear none of it.

"I mean, *damn*, is it so hard to just be professional about it?" he started to sound firmer in his tone. Not angry, just deeply, intensely serious.

"Now, Kelly," Trinity tried to add. But I had more to say first. This wasn't her fight.

"Kelly, I *swear* I didn't mean to. I got caught up in a—"

"A what?" he prodded.

My head sank. "A *dream*, alright? It's silly. It's so stupid."

He chuckled, but not at all in a fun way. "Of *course*. See, I knew this was a risk, but... You're just... you're too freaking awkward around guys for this ever to work."

He'd slung that accusation at me in the past, but it especially hurt this time. I wasn't about to just take it.

"And maybe you're too distant toward everyone, you know? There's those girls at the club that freaking adore you, but you never talk to them! Why is that? Maybe you're afraid too!"

He pointed directly at me. "So you admit it! You *are* afraid!"

"Oh yeah?" I shouted back at him, pent up with frustration. "At least *I* have a date this week. With a charming, outgoing, caring *man*!"

Kelly stopped, certainly not expecting me to say that.

"You... have a date?" he asked sheepishly.

"YOU HAVE A DATE??" Trinity squealed from behind me, badly failing to read the room.

Kelly stood there for a moment, still a little stunned. I didn't plan on telling him tonight, if ever. But my anger forced it out of me. Instead of lashing back or convincing me otherwise, he lowered his voice and his temper evened up.

"Well then I guess you win," was all he said.

Kelly looked over to Trinity who was beyond confused by my accidental kiss, the sudden return to fighting, the date reveal... everything. "I'm sorry for causing trouble. It's happened too many times."

Kelly then glanced over to me, my heart racing from equal parts stress and exhilaration. "Good luck on your date."

He returned to the house where I presume he'd grab his clothes and head straight to his car. Trinity and I stood in silence for a few moments. Again, I noticed the beautiful, twinkling fairy lights above us. But the magic was gone. The whole garden felt like a goddamn murder scene.

FOR AS BAD as I felt after the pool fiasco, I felt even worse in the aftermath of this fight. Not because of some unrealized, botched attempt to kiss Kelly – as strange as the whole thing was. But the fact that I practically ensured Kelly would never come to this house ever again. No more handiwork, no more photoshoots, no more anything. As far as I could tell, after that, he was out of our lives for good.

Trinity tried to take some of the blame for 'heating things up' with her requests, but I insisted it wasn't her fault. I let my crazy dream come to life and for that, I deserve the blame. Plus, despite what seemed like undeniably chemistry for a moment, the fight all but confirmed Kelly and I are – and always have been – a terrible fit. I'm awkward, frazzled, and my identity is completely in flux. He's cold, distant, and most importantly: *straight*. I refused to address it and went right to bed to sleep off my frustration.

WITH ALL THE CRAZY RESPONSIBILITIES, shoots, and life events, I'd completely forgotten that Trinity was finally due to get her soft cast and sling removed at the doctor today. I woke up early, groggy from the few glasses of wine I had the night before. Drinking was never really my thing, and damn was that fact rearing its ugly head.

Notably, I did wake up to a text from an unknown number, which I quickly realized was Bryce, asking me if I wanted to meet for drinks at a place called Calcifer's this coming Saturday. He even told me he'd pick me up. The gesture was so kind that, just for a moment, relieved my hangover. I returned the text, accepting his offer.

"Are you coming, Andie!?" Trinity yelled, knocking loudly on my bedroom door. "Let's go! We're gonna be late!"

Yep, there's that headache again...

While we didn't really talk about the Kelly fight, Trinity demanded I tell her everything about the upcoming date, about how I saw Bryce for the first time at the tennis tournament, how we shot eyes at each other, and how he ultimately asked me to the Golden Dunes Ball... *through* Tara.

"Well it's certainly not traditional... But I'm really happy it's a yes!"

"A conditional yes," I reminded her. "As long as he can 'sweep me off my feet' on Saturday." I never cared for that phrase, but it was apt. We both laughed. Her questions about Bryce and everything else boy-related continued into the doctor's office waiting room. I did my best to answer with what little information I had.

The appointment was more or less a formality. By now, Trinity was pretty much back to normal. Her face had healed almost 100% and she'd been lifting light objects with previously injured body parts on the regular. Even the doctor himself was impressed by her progress.

"Now I'm not saying you're a medical *miracle*," he began, wrapping up his evaluation. "But not many people are able to bounce back this fluidly."

"Lots of credit to this one," Trinity said, grabbing my hand as her humility shined through. "My perfect little home helper."

The doctor smiled. "Family's important. Sometimes just as important as the treatments themselves."

Trinity and I rolled our eyes at his cheesy line, which he too recognized.

"Alright, alright. Well, I'm comfortable letting you remove all slings and braces. I recommend a few PT sessions before returning to high intensity activities like swimming, but consider your light day-to-day activities unimpeded."

This was fantastic news! The correlation between her physical restrictions and mental health was obvious, so a clean bill of health was exactly what the doctor ordered – for lack of a better phrase. He wished her luck, leaving us with instructions and recommendations for a physical therapist.

"So how are we celebrating?" I asked. "Maybe a trip to MooMoo's? Or maybe I film your triumphant return to Princess Trinity."

Her face lit up. "Definitely MooMoo's! But we also got shipped these fun, flirty red dresses I want us to try on. Oh! And I have all these ideas for a new 'twinning' series to start."

I sat there for a moment, hanging on the word 'twinning'.

"Or, you know... We just turn the channel back to you? No need to keep *me* around, right?"

By the look of it, Trinity was certain I was joking. "What? You're kidding. Princess Trinity's growth has, what, *tripled* since Andie came on board? Let's just keep that train rolling!"

The numbers don't lie. The growth of her Instagram, TikTok, and even Facebook pages were undeniable. And yes, a lot of that credit went to me. But a lot of it also went to Kelly.

"I've been thinking... With Kelly gone and that whole fake boyfriend thing in the past... Maybe we call it a day on Online Andie."

Credit to Trinity, she's always been unquestionably supportive of my decisions. Opinionated, yes, but always supportive.

"You don't want to be Andie anymore?"

"I just... I think I should focus on other life things now, you know?" I said frankly. "My job, this date... hell, my *career*. I have an exam I need to be prepared for."

She was clearly stressing every muscle in her body to prevent showing disappointment. "I hope this doesn't have anything to do with Kelly. It was a lapse of judgment, but that doesn't define you."

I confidently shook my head, though I knew deep down he played a little part in this decision. My stupid, impulsive self played a real role in scaring him off. "I think it's just time I move on from this era, you know?"

"Uh-huh..." was all Trinity managed to say. Though she barely showed it, I could tell every ounce of her energy went toward looking unfazed.

Despite receiving the best medical news of the last couple months, we left the hospital in silence. Trinity didn't want to talk about the club, about Princess Trinity, or about *anything* for that matter. The ride home was dead quiet. And when I brought up MooMoo's again to celebrate, she told me she'd lost her appetite.

Physically, Trinity was pretty much back to normal. Her skin was healed and vibrant once again. Her bones and limbs needed strengthening, but were healed. Mentally however, Trinity wasn't there. Pulling back from Princess Trinity looked like it hit her hard. But pulling back was something I felt like I had to do in order to grow. With no more Princess Trinity work, my life and career were back in focus. All I could do now was hope she'd magically get over it.

THE FOLLOWING week was particularly unique, considering I had not one, not two, but *three* private lessons booked with Janice. God knows why, but something must have lit a fire under her butt wanting to improve. Not only was she busting her ass more than usual, but the chit chat was kept to a minimum, and our lessons were streamlined, focused, and productive. The extra money from the lessons was nice, but the distraction from my at-home tension with Trinity was even more valuable.

Maybe 'tension' is the wrong word, but there was an objective change in Trinity's demeanor after declaring my retirement from 'Online Andie'. She wasn't rude, angry, or even unpleasant, but her motivation bottomed out and the active, upbeat aunt I'd grown to love had taken a step back.

Sure I felt a little bad, but it was a forward-looking decision I knew was best for me. Kelly was gone. Trinity was all healed up. My services to Princess Trinity were no longer needed. But of course, I still wanted her in my life. So once Saturday rolled around and we were in the hours leading up to my date, I knocked on her bedroom door.

"Hey, I'm gonna start getting ready soon. Bryce is picking me up in two hours. Wanna help me pick out a look?"

It was silent for a minute behind the closed door while she considered. "No, I'm okay, thanks," she said, gloomily. "You've got good taste. I know you'll pick out something cute."

Her words were kind but her energy felt dead. Ask me a little over a week ago, and I would've bet Trinity was incapable of denying an opportunity to help someone get dolled up – particularly me, going on my first *real* date.

"Suit yourself..." I answered, admittedly disappointed.

The next couple hours were spent alone, doing my hair, makeup, and picking an outfit for what Bryce said was a 'swanky vibe'. Over the last couple months, I'd amassed an incredible amount of women's clothing – enough to have multiple options for any occasion. Knowing nothing about Calcifer's beyond Bryce's 'swanky' description, I took a stab with a relatively conservative, semi-formal black dress, 3-inch heels, and some simple silver jewelry. I brought back out the curling iron for some long, loose waves – some of which I clipped back for a cute, half-up, half-down wavy ponytail look. For some extra feminine flair, I added some large black ribbon and tied it into a bow to the back of my hair. I finished off my look with some very basic makeup, a spritz of perfume, and a matching black purse.

I looked and felt gorgeous staring at myself in the living room mirror, waiting for Bryce to arrive any minute now, but mostly wishing Trinity would come out to geek out over my look.

"I'm heading out soon!" I called out to Trinity, who was still in her bedroom with the door shut.

Of course, I hoped she'd emerge to take a look at my outfit, but clearly that wasn't gonna happen.

"Have fun, be safe!" was all she said back.

A few seconds later my phone dinged with a text from Bryce, telling me he was parked outside. For a moment, I wondered why he wasn't coming to the door to get me, but maybe that's asking too much. I responded that I'd just be a minute.

I'm not sure why, but I needed a moment to hype myself up. I needed to remind myself that this was indeed a normal, healthy thing to do. Of everything I'd done this summer, this was maybe the biggest step. Not only was I going on a date with a boy, but I was basically going on a date with a boy and *presenting feminine*. I only wish Trinity was next to me to calm my nerves and remind me that, *yes*, this is good for me. That this is something I want. But again, maybe I'm asking too much...

Bravely, I stepped out onto the porch into the dark. The house lights softly lighting up the front yard, but everything was overwhelmed by the harsh headlights of Bryce's car.

I think most of me was hoping for a normal, casual date. But taking one look at his car proved otherwise. The boy was in a sleek, matte black Ferrari.

Something was telling me this night would be anything but normal.

17

I'd never been a person to be overly impressed with wealth. It just wasn't in my DNA. But even relatively modest people can't help but lose their breath a *little* in the presence of a Ferrari.

There wasn't even a need to reach for the door handle as the moment I did, the car door swung up like a futuristic spaceship. And sitting inside that spaceship, awaiting my entrance, was my date for the night, Bryce.

"*Sick*, right?" he said with a little smile. No 'hi' or 'hello', strangely. There he sat in the driver's seat, his platinum blonde hair in a cool crew cut and wearing a black blazer, black pants, and for some reason, sunglasses.

I chuckled, assuming he was playing up the luxury just a bit. "Shades at night?"

"They're brand new," he said, plainly. "Plus, they fit the car. Come on, get in!"

I took my seat in the car as the spaceship door shut automatically beside me, making a cool, techy beep sound as it locked. Already, I was getting a sense of Bryce's over-the-top 'rich boy swagger'.

I know I told myself to keep expectations low for the date, but it's pretty hard to do so tooling around in a quarter million dollar car driven by a guy wearing sunglasses at night. Not to mention, someone who was two years younger than me and fresh out of prep school.

Not entirely sure what to say to him, we made small talk about the car the entire 15 minute drive there. I couldn't help but feel like I was back at GDCC for the 4th of July fireworks. All summer I'd been alternating my hats between 'worker' and 'member's guest'. Tonight was certainly the latter, evidenced by the stares the car garnered at each and every stop sign and stop light in town. A unique experience, and one I wasn't entirely sure how to feel about.

The luxurious, bougie energy only heightened upon pulling up to Calcifer's. I immediately understood what he meant by 'swanky'. A sleek, metallic sign out front with the restaurant's name written in barely legible cursive, both water *and* fire elements surrounding the building, and a valet service of eager young guys fighting over who'd get to park Bryce's car. He casually tossed one of the boys the keys and full of country club cockiness, led us into the restaurant.

The host escorted us to the bar where we were seated and swiftly greeted by the bartender.

"Mr. Fox, good evening!" the obsequious man said with a

nervous smile, then turned toward me. "And good evening to the lady as well."

I blushed upon being called a lady – understandably so, considering my outfit. Bryce didn't even wait for my order, promptly ordering two gin and tonics.

"Bryce Fox? Quite the name."

He shrugged, still not overly chatty. "You know, it's just a name. But I guess I dig it."

Okay...

His entire being felt so out of place. His fancy clothes, the quarter million dollar car, the shades which he *finally* took off when we got to our seats... And all at 18. What kind of guy *is* this?

"Don't take this the wrong way, but can you even legally order drinks? Not that I'm 21 either."

Bryce calmly shook his head. "Doesn't matter here. My dad's an investor so they're paid to be chill."

The obsequious bartender returned in record time, handing us two beautifully garnished gin and tonics. Bryce held up his glass and offered 'cheers'. We clinked.

"Yummy!" I noted, sipping my drink a few times while mentally searching for something to bring up.

I know, I'll admit it. I'm bad on dates. And over the next 20 minutes, that was clear as day. I made ill-timed jokes, paused between questions and answers, checked my phone a few too many times... But even someone as socially inept as myself couldn't deserve all the blame here.

I tried talking about tennis – our one commonality – but he wasn't interested. I asked him questions about fencing, his prep school days, and his thoughts on New Jersey versus Michigan... but he was so... "over it".

Something about Bryce just felt *off*. He didn't ask any questions about me and only wanted to talk about his possessions or things his dad did and said. A couple times I tried to bring up nursing, he scoffed at the profession, either saying the earning potential wasn't high enough or it sounded too boring.

Every time he opened his mouth, it felt like a new, negative box was getting checked off. It's almost like this date was going... well, kinda *bad*.

"So you're close with your father?" I asked, trying to be as engaging as possible. Full, steady eye contact, hoping to reel him back in.

"He does a lot for me. He does a lot for everyone."

I grunted internally, fed up with his constantly short, unengaging answers.

"Uh huh, yeah," I said a little too dismissively. Though suddenly, after being undisturbed the entirety of our evening – except by the bartender of course – a girl approached me from behind.

"I'm so sorry..." she began timidly. The girl couldn't have been older than 16. Both Bryce and I turned to her. Me, smiling. Bryce, shooting her an annoyed glare. "You're Andie. From Princess Trinity?"

Holy shit... Was I getting *recognized*?

"Uh, heh, yeah, I am!" I replied cheerfully, though certainly caught off guard.

"Princess Trinity?" Bryce asked. "What's that?"

The girl's attention turned to Bryce, giggling. "Like you don't know? I promise I won't tell, but it's an honor to meet 'Mystery Man'."

Bryce looked deathly confused. "*Mystery* man... What the fuck are you talking about?"

I held my hand out to get him to quiet down and read-dressed the girl. "I'm actually stepping back from the page soon. Princess Trinity herself will be taking back over! But thank you so much for liking our content and I'm honored to have you as a fan!"

As politely as possible, I shooed away the girl. Suddenly, Bryce was a lot more engaged. But still, not too kindly and more accusatory.

"Wait, what was she talking about? You have a *boyfriend*?"

"No no no, it's, uh..." Hmm, how to summarize my last couple months without sounding like a crazy person... "I help out with my aunt's beauty product social media personality. It's all a performance though. And we had a 'Mystery Man' be my pretend boyfriend. Again, *all* a performance."

Bryce looked concerned. "Well who is he?"

"I, uh... I can't say."

"Why not?" he prodded.

Well *now* I was starting to feel a little intruded upon.

"Because it's not my business to share, okay? He's a good guy who just likes his privacy. That's why we never showed his face."

He stared at the ceiling for a moment, then took a sip of his drink. "I picked you as my date because I assumed you weren't seeing anyone else."

Assumed? Why? I wanted to ask him, but figured doing so would only make more of a scene than we already were.

I'm not sure if it was the girl's interruption or the re-emergence of Kelly into my mind thinking about Mystery Man, but Bryce's attitude was really starting to rub me the wrong way. I mean, hell, my date with *Kelly* was so much more natural, fluid and fun. And that was a *fake* date.

"I'm gonna use the restroom, okay?" I said firmly, sliding my cell phone into my purse and placing it on the bar. "I'd like you to settle up and call me an uber please."

Without a word from Bryce, I walked off to the bathroom. The whole night of forced conversation, needless flexing, and sudden defensiveness. I really just wanted to be home. I wanted to come home, hash it out with Trinity, and go back to the safe, friendly way things were.

I can't believe I'm saying this, but I'd really have loved to tell Kelly about this. I'm sure he'd get a huge kick out of how snobby and obnoxious Bryce was acting. A terrible case of 'member-itis', as he once put it.

My mind was so jumbled that I barely even registered going into the women's bathroom – a *public* women's restroom – for the first time ever. It just came naturally to me dressed like I am.

I returned to the bar where Bryce looked peeved. Clearly, things didn't go how he planned.

"You called my uber?" I prompted him, having calmed down a bit but still feeling upset.

He nodded. "Three minutes away." I grabbed my phone and purse on the counter and followed him out the door. We waited there together in front of the still-eager valet guys. According to Bryce's phone, it was one minute away.

"Look, Andie," he began. "I might've been kind of an asshole, okay? I still need you as my date to the ball."

I rolled my eyes. "Really? After tonight, do you *really* think that's a good idea? I don't think we really match, Bryce. I'm sorry."

Again, he got defensive. "What, are you gonna take your boyfriend?"

"Jesus Christ, Bryce, *no*. He's not my boyfriend, and honestly, I don't think I'm gonna go at all."

Bryce huffed, frustrated, but visibly trying to calm himself.

"Look, can I be honest? I *need* a date. All the girls at the club... The summers I've been here... they don't like me. I just... They all think I'm some kind of rich snob."

Finally, a little self-awareness. "And you think you're not?"

"None of the real girls will go with me, and my Dad... he said he won't stand for his son not having a date."

I was *this* close to lashing out at him over use of the term 'real girls', but right at that moment, the uber pulled up. I was so freaking done with tonight.

"Goodnight Bryce," I said, stepping toward the car.

He let me walk for just a moment before shouting out. "Wait! Andie."

I'm not sure why, but I turned around to give him one last chance to redeem himself. "*What*?"

"You wanna be a nurse, right? Well my dad knows every president at all the big hospitals in Chicago. Come with me to the dance, and I'll make sure you get any job you want. Any place, any pay, any position."

I stopped dead in my tracks, and told the uber driver I needed a second.

"Your dad... He could do that?" I asked coolly.

He shrugged. "It's a *nursing* job, Andie. And he's got crazy powerful friends. It'd be literally nothing to him."

Every bone in my body knew how shifty this felt. But if I learned anything about the country club folks around here, it's that they play by different rules. And sometimes to get ahead, you simply have to use what you got... and take that leap of faith.

"It's one night, and you're done," Bryce reiterated.

I stared at him with a grimace. "Fine. I'll go. *One* night."

18

To say my feelings were 'mixed' would be an understatement. Fresh off the first date of my entire life – and a *bad* one – I found myself with both the opportunity of a lifetime and a stomach-gurgling second date with a certified spoiled pick.

Nothing about this was particularly calming. For someone who took so much comfort in living a drama-free life, my recent actions were proving to be the opposite.

I decided not to tell Trinity about the date – or at least about the main parts. But that proved to be not much of an issue, because when I got home, she asked no follow-up questions beyond 'have a nice time?'. Easy enough, I suppose.

The most difficult part of everything was how trapped I felt. Trapped between desires, interests, and what I felt was necessary to succeed in life. I did a hell of a lot this summer – *much* more than I thought I'd do. I was the errand boy for my injured aunt. I worked an increasingly time-consuming part-time job. I became a shockingly successful social media influencer. And of course, I've been doing my absolute best to focus on my studies.

But on top of all of that fluff, I'd discovered, explored, and eventually embraced a brand new feminine side of me. Wearing girls' clothing and makeup, first in private, but eventually in public. Adopting a female version of my name that I grew quite fond of. There were even more intimate, private changes like shaving my body, posing in the mirror in lingerie, and fantasizing about relations with a strong, sexy man.

None of these things, I thought, would be inherently harmful. And yet, when all is said and done, pursuing these desires have brought drama, pain, and ruin to my life. Bad dates, ruined friendships, disappointed relatives. Why does it have to be this way? Why does it have to be a trade off? *Why* must the euphoria of exploring my gender come at a cost?

None of these questions had simple answers, and straining my brain for those answers only made me more frustrated and depressed. Was all of this self-exploration even worth it? Bryce – for all his faults – was right about me. I'm *not* a 'real girl'. And thinking otherwise is a fool's errand. Girls like me... we're always going to be the last pick of the draft.

I knew that I wouldn't be able to fall asleep without making a bargain with myself. I needed some closure, or at least a solid placeholder emotion that'd get me through the week. Something that would keep me from going insane from the conflicted feelings.

And so I decided on this: for the remainder of the week, there'd be no Andie. No dresses, no skirts, no bras, no panties.

No shaving, no moisturizing, and especially no imagining myself with any men. I'd present and act as a confident, straight male. Not because I believe that I actually *am*, but because I believe that I *have* to be.

But the night of the ball, for one night only, I will re-emerge as Andie. I'll do everything I can to give Bryce the evening he needs. But after the ball, once my deal with Bryce is done and I have my job, I can set up my new life in Chicago with a passing grade on the NCLEX, a nice apartment, and a drama-free, *male* existence. Leaving all this stupid, wastefulness behind.

THE DECISION to deliberately suppress my true self wasn't easy – especially the morning after my date, cursed with a stress-hang-over from the night before. But things stung a little bit less as the week went by. And that's what it's all about, right? Taking things day by day?

Things were back to being friendly with Trinity, though the charismatic spark we once shared hadn't returned. We still ate breakfast together, made small talk about the town, work, and other things. She did carry on with Princess Trinity posting, though she notably wasn't jumping out of her seat to show off the new products or outfits she was gifted.

I took things *super* easy this week. Scheduled for only a single tennis shift on Tuesday, I was able to spend the majority of my week on important, forward-facing things like exam prep. With Trinity to care for as well as no feminine self-care, shaving, makeup, or worrying about my outfits, I was suddenly swimming in time. I even made my return to the town library for the first time in well over a month.

I spotted many library regulars from early summer and every so often, I'd catch one doing a double take – probably thinking 'ugh, that guy who spreads out papers all over the table is back...'.

It's funny... With three, four, or five days of growing out my body hair, I was starting to look less like a girl and more like how I'd always looked – still *feminine*, but much more obviously male. So I knew the looks I got *couldn't* be due to thinking I'm a girl. Simply the recognition of a familiar face, then back to ignoring me to carry out their days.

In fact, everyone in town seemed to be living their lives as normal. Lower-income locals living amongst the high-income tourists. I used to wonder constantly what they thought about the disparity in livelihoods. But now regardless of who walked by, I'd feel a bit envious. Envious none of them felt the constant pull between genders that I did. I simply had to keep reminding myself that with time, I'd feel better. It only takes time.

Admittedly, my nights were less joyous than they used to be. I didn't realize until now how 'in the moment' I'd lived all summer. For the entire past week, I've lived my life looking ahead. Thinking about the *upcoming* exam. Perusing the internet for an *upcoming* apartment. Picturing my *fast-approaching* life in Chicago... *as a man*. Gone were the days of sitting back and relaxing with Trinity, painting our nails, trying on clothes, and talking about our lives as we were living them in the *moment*. Not some sort of nebulous, bleak future. For a while there, I got quite good at living in the joy of today.

I think I even spooked Trinity a bit with my forward-looking changes and sudden abandonment of femininity. Peeking over my shoulder while scrolling Zillow on my laptop always garnered a 'huff'. And though she never directly *said* anything, I think the small bits of facial and body hair returning to my body made her considerably sadder.

The summer – and our time together – was ending. And there was nothing she or I could do about it...

I WENT BACK and forth between excitement and dread for the night of the Golden Dunes Ball. On the one hand, I had to accompany a truly dreadful, spoiled recent prep school grad as his date. For hours on end, he'd escort me around, showing me off as if I were nothing but a plaything, purely for the purposes of getting the 'respect' of his father for finding a date. My expectations were lower than dirt.

And yet... I was given my final night of femininity. Though only out of necessity, knowing anything more would further torpedo my life and exacerbate my problems. Still, Friday night, I dreamed soft, delicate, feminine dreams. I dreamed I was getting spun around on the dance floor, my dress twirling and my bouncy, feminine curls flying around my head and on my shoulders. And spinning me around? The same, strong, faceless man as before. I now know that my subconscious assumed it was Kelly, but I suppose my subconscious also made a correction. Because my dream man was faceless once more, and honestly, that was better for me. After all, how can you hurt a faceless man?

I wasted the afternoon away, procrastinating getting ready and taking frequent walks up, down, and around Lumber Lane hoping to clear my head. It didn't help. Tonight was too important. I have to be the perfect date. I have to be charming. For Bryce. For my career. For *me*. No better time than the present, I thought after ditzing around for hours on end, simultaneously dreading and anticipating the night ahead.

Over the months, I'd found taking a hot, soothing bath to be one of the best remedies for calming my nerves. Of course, I was quite spoiled with all the fun, foofy bathing products we were gifted for Princess Trinity. I wonder if things hadn't been cut short, if we'd have gone as far as doing a *bath-themed* series of pictures and videos.

Nevertheless, this bath was for both relaxation *and* productivity. In the spirit of becoming Andie one final time, I meticulously shaved my entire body. Legs, underarms, the small bits of facial hair I'd let grow throughout the week and, yes, even my private areas. I mean, I'm going all out, aren't I?

I tried hard not to allow myself too much euphoria with the shaving or moisturizing with oils and lotions. But damn, did I miss this... There's an undeniable joy one gets knowing their body is soft, smooth, and feminine. But enough self-indulgence. I still had much more to do.

In the interest of getting ample drying time, I painted my nails soon after leaving the tub. While not initially in the plan, I must've accidentally left one bottle in my room after my clothing purge. It was a pretty, light orange color that looked lovely next to my skin tone.

I kept my hair straight and my makeup relatively simple, harkening back to the several times Trinity gushed over how beautiful I looked with just a little bit of makeup. Foundation, concealer, mascara, and just the faintest, light-red lipstick. The dress I'd held aside had similar energy. A long, reddish-orange evening gown, it felt close to something a girl a few years younger than me might wear to prom or a homecoming dance. The 3-inch heels gave me just enough lift to feel formally feminine, but not threaten Bryce's masculinity.

Tucked in my bedroom closet and buried in a mini chest was a selection of golden jewelry items. These drudged up another memory of my dressing with Trinity. If my memory serves, this was the first jewelry I wore unnecessarily – meaning not for the purpose of selling or reviewing a product, and simply for fun. At the time, I remember thinking that was so special.

The only thing missing was perfume. And yes, of *course* the first one I could find was *Mystique* – the original scent from my shoot with Kelly. Even putting a few conservative spritzes on my wrists and neck made the memories rush back in. The way he welcomed me onto the couch to straddle him. The way I, for the first time ever, felt a hint of attraction toward the male body. The way I teased him by kissing his chest... a spontaneous decision that led to one of our most-viewed Princess Trinity videos and ushered in Andie's 'mystery man' era. An era I'd have to force myself to forget.

Boy, how the time flew... I checked my phone and noticed

that I had only 10 or so minutes to spare until Bryce picked me up. In the Ferrari, I assume, knowing him.

What I really needed now wasn't validation or a confidence boost. It was something to settle my stomach. Some crackers or nuts or anything that would help avoid the growing pit in my gut. Fortunately, I found some Saltines in the cabinet. In my estimation, the perfect dry-as-a-bone stomach-settling snack.

The kitchen was quiet. Trinity in her room, me at the table, carefully munching some crackers, trying my best not to ruin my lipstick. I couldn't believe this was it. This was how my journey in girlhood would end? A dolled-up, glam look in a prom dress with a shitty guy, and then never again?

I heard Trinity's door open down the hall and froze.

Shit. She must not know I'm out here. Sure enough, she stopped in her tracks the moment she saw me at the table.

Her eyes widened, though not from fear. She looked a mix of confused, disappointed and... dare I say, *annoyed*?

"Hey," was all she said.

"Hi," I replied, still with crackers in my mouth. I didn't know what to tell her back. She knew about my date tonight. She knew all about the Ball. Hell, she's *attended* several in the past. Any lingering chance she'd be attending tonight was put to bed, evidenced by her sweatpants, lack of makeup, and messy top bun.

She quietly walked past me and went to the kitchen, noticing the open Saltines box. "Good snack," she said mindlessly. "He's picking you up soon?"

"A few minutes, yeah." The awkwardness stung. *God* was it unbearable...

Trinity gave a quick nod with no eye contact as she made her way back down the hall with a handful of crackers. "Well, have a fun last night of being Andie."

"Trinity, wait," I called out, right before she shut the door. "Do you really have no opinions on my outfit?"

She looked at me indifferently. "It's nice. You got pretty good at this stuff."

"You know, *you* could dress up too. You don't need a date for these things."

She rolled her eyes. "I've been to many more than you, Anderson. I *think* I know that..."

There she went, calling me *Anderson*... "Why not go? You loved the fourth of July."

Again, she passively shrugged. "Not feeling it."

This 'sad girl' bullshit was starting to really annoy me. I mean, goddamn it, my last night of being Andie and she *still* doesn't care?

"Okay, I'm sorry," I said to her firmly. "Is it me? Did I do something wrong? Because ever since I told you I wasn't down for dressing up anymore, you've been acting like you don't give a shit about me."

Trinity looked insulted and also a little surprised. I'd never yelled at her like that before.

"Excuse me? Andie, it's *you* who's been acting like you don't give a shit. Not wearing clothing you obviously *want* to wear and not taking care of yourself?"

"Who says I want to wear them?" I snapped back at her. "They're *your* clothes anyway. Princess *TRINITY*. *Not* Princess *ANDIE*."

"So then why tonight, huh? So you can impress some guy you clearly don't care much about? And *yeah*, Andie, I'm getting that sense."

"Why do you say that?"

"Because you never talk about him!"

"You never ask! You don't even care about my life! You just wanted me to wear your clothes and be your little *daughter*, huh? Well it's been fucking blowing up my life!" My last few words were as loud as I've said anything to her for our entire relationship. Trinity noticed this too, and backed down just a bit.

Trinity looked at me somberly. "You know, I've been around a while," she began, much more quietly. "Too many times I've been blamed for shit that's not my fault. I'm not gonna let *you* do that too."

The air was still. This was a whole new Trinity I was dealing with.

"Vince, my ex. Remember him? I told you we split up because he blamed me for shit I couldn't control. There was a lot wrong with that relationship, Anderson. But I thought if just *one* particular thing went right, maybe we could fix it, settle down, and live out our lives in peace."

I sat there, calmly, not sure what to say. "What do you mean?"

"No, I never had kids, Anderson. So you'll have to excuse me if some of my 'distance' comes off as bad parenting or what-ever... But I *was* pregnant with a daughter. Actually, three daughters. And every one I miscarried. Every. Single. FUCK-ING! ONE!!!"

Her screams shook me. This Trinity was totally uncharted and more intense than I'd ever seen her before. More intense than I'd ever seen *anyone* before.

"Vince wanted no part of someone who couldn't help carry on his legacy. I mean, fuck, I can't even carry on my *own* legacy..." She sighed deeply and leaned up against the hallway wall, letting her energy levels reset. "So yeah, excuse me if I got a little too excited about another daughter... And a little too miserable when I started losing my fourth, Anderson."

I couldn't believe the tension. I didn't even know how to feel, much less what to say. The weight of hte moment was unbearable but got broken up with a knock at the door.

"Hmm. At least he came to the door like a *real* man this time," Trinity scoffed, then turned around and went into her bedroom, leaving me in silence.

19

The pit in my stomach from my fight with Trinity didn't get much better being around Bryce, considering he himself was a walking, talking pile of discomfort.

"I got it washed. Did you notice?" Bryce said, attempting to break the silence in the car. We'd been driving for almost 10 minutes now with barely any conversation.

"That car?" I asked.

"The Ferrari."

I groaned. "No, I didn't notice. It's a black car. Usually they don't show dirt."

He shrugged, conceding the point. At least he wasn't obnoxiously chatty this time. I think he and I both knew this was a marriage of convenience anyway. More than anything, I just wanted to get this night over with.

THE DESERT-THEMED GLAMOUR of Golden Dunes Country Club was in full force tonight, and that was evident the moment we reached the guard gate. A friendly tip of the cap from the guard as he tried to hide his gawking at Bryce's car, prompting a smirk. I guess flashing daddy's money never gets old.

The GDCC Ball was a black tie event through and through. Not a soul around wasn't dressed to the nines. The men in sharp black tuxedos and the ladies (and me, I suppose) wearing fancy ball gowns with their hair and makeup all done-up for the special night. Everything from the entrance to the parking lot to the exterior and interior decorations leading to the ballroom were legitimately impressive.

"Why are you so quiet? You said you'd be a good date. That's part of the deal." Bryce said, holding out his arm to escort me through the halls.

I reluctantly linked my arm with his. Obviously, *Trinity* was on my mind. Not him. But I wasn't about to tell this shitty guy about my troubles and project any vulnerability. So I forced a smile, and looked him in the eye. "I'll be good."

Bryce nodded proudly, as if his stern warning was what fixed my attitude. "Let's mingle. I want everyone to know I have a date."

It was strange seeing the ballroom actually being used for, well, a *ball*. Up until tonight, I'd really only seen it used for storage, registration lines, aerobics classes for old ladies... Really anything *but* a ball. But tonight it was totally decked out. A massive chandelier hung from the center of the room, scattering twinkling light all around the massive room. At the head of the ballroom, a 12-piece band – complete with a singer plus a rhythm and horn section – played upbeat jazz tunes to the amusement of the members.

Aside from the massive, mostly unoccupied dance floor (to be fair, it's early in the night), the remainder of the ballroom was reserved for dining space, with first-come-first-serve seating at the dozens of delectably decorated dining tables. And of *course*, I have to mention how the entire ballroom was lined with food and drink stations serving anything from fancy-looking chicken fingers to delicacies like foie gras and even jellyfish. Each station was manned by a sleekly-dressed GDCC employee, putting on their happiest, most obsequious faces.

Aesthetically, everything was perfect. I glanced around for Tara, hoping to compliment her planning and execution skills on an event this large. Almost certainly, she was in the back, sweating away and praying things didn't fall apart. Admittedly, I also glanced around for Kelly, who I still hadn't seen since the disastrous blow-up. As much as I wanted to talk to him and just be in his company, I knew he'd just roast me for accompanying an uppity member to GDCC's most lavish night of the year. But he must not be working tonight.

Over the next half hour, Bryce figuratively – and at points *literally* – dragged me around the ballroom to meet old, rich folks who mostly referred to him as 'Fox's son' or 'Dave's boy'. It was obvious that beyond proving to his acquaintances that he had a date, he had little interest in involving me in the actual conversation. Still, I kept my head down and remained pretty and polite.

"Can we take a break and get some food?" I asked him after probably the eighth straight introduction. "It's either gonna get cold or they'll take it away."

He glanced at my stomach and the somewhat form-fitting dress. "You wanna be bloated? We haven't even seen my dad yet."

Ugh, I hate this guy. "Can we see him *now* then?"

Bryce shook his head. "Dad never gets here until late. It's a bad look to get here too early."

For a moment there, I almost wanted to toss my drink in his face and storm out of the party, fed up with his ego and attitude. But I knew if I just held out a little longer, I could make a good impression with his powerful father, get my job, and walk out of here a free girl... er, uh, *guy*.

Eventually – only once *Bryce* was hungry – did we make our way over to the food stations. Not knowing the next time he'd 'allow' me to eat, I filled up my plate the best I could, thanking the staff with each dish I added to my plate. I think a few of them recognized me, either from the 4th of July event or from walking around the tennis courts. Even though the staff didn't look *too* stressed, I couldn't help but feel a little judged for being on the other side tonight.

Bryce and I were definitely on the later half of dining considering by the time we sat down to eat, many had left for the dance floor. We ate alone together as he rambled off stories of different wealthy, powerful members who were present tonight. But still, no sight of his father. I looked longingly at the dance floor, conflicted. Part of me wanted to get up, dance, and have a fun rest of the night. But unfortunately it had to be with Bryce.

"Let me get another drink and we'll hop on the dance floor. I'm sure there's more people around to show you off to." Bryce shot up from his seat and went to fetch a drink for himself – *without* asking me what I wanted. This fucking guy...

Though I'll say, the brief minute or two he was away from me felt like bliss. I actually got to soak in the ambiance and appreciate the privilege of attending an event like this. Many girls – er, *guys* – aren't this lucky. Tiny blessings, I suppose.

"Hey!" I heard a couple people approach from behind. It was a group of girls, one of which I recognized – Allie, the brunette lifeguard I met in the break room months ago.

"Hey, I know you..." she muttered, then whispered to a friend of hers. "*Shit*. Grace wasn't kidding."

It was immediately obvious she was drunk and the filter was off for tonight. *Lucky me...*

"Grace?" I asked. "Sorry, it's been a minute."

"Are you... like, trans or something?" Allie asked.

I turned red, a little put off by her bluntness. Thankfully, her friend jumped in. "You can't *say* that, Allie. It's insulting!" her friend turned back to me. "Sorry, she's a little drunk."

I didn't know what to be upset about. The rude interruption, the drunk accusation, or the fact that her friend considered 'trans' an insult."

"I'm, uh... I'm here with Bryce," I replied, choosing to ignore her rudeness.

The blonde friend looked at me funny. "Bryce *Fox*? Oh, shit..." again, she quickly clocked that maybe I wasn't here with

him against my will. "I mean, that's nice. His family's, uh...
cool!"

Clearly there was nothing more to say to these girls, as they
gave me a quick 'see you around' before escorting drunk Allie
away and leaving me be.

Well, *shit*... As if I couldn't feel any worse about tonight. A
not-so-subtle reminder that being a girl was an utter, complete
waste of my time.

Bryce returned with his drink and swiftly led us to the
dance floor. But no, not to *dance*. To schmooze. He wanted to
have me linked by the arm, trotting me around like some sort
of impressive item. Funny, after several months of trans-
forming myself on and off, trying to look as pretty and desirable as possible, tonight I simply couldn't feel more the
opposite.

Meeting rich folks, laughing at the same jokes over and over
again, pretending like I knew their references... it was starting
to drive me crazy. I felt alone, but also suffocated. I desperately
needed space from this man. But each time I tried to walk away,
he gripped my arm firmer, reminding me of our deal.

"Andie, I need you next to me," he insisted, even slurring his
words a bit now.

"Everyone's seen me with you. Do you seriously need a date
at all times?"

He considered my point for a moment. Or maybe he just
recognized my frustration. "Let's dance then." I took the
bargain, knowing that at least I wouldn't have to talk to anyone
new while dancing.

The song was slow and romantic. Couples filled the dance

floor, swaying back and forth, laughing, and having their intimate moments.

We did just a simple, swaying dance, but it resulted in my face being far closer to Bryce's than I'd ever want it to be.

"Thank you for coming," he said softly, a weak attempt at 'charm'. I didn't buy it for a second though. I just wanted to meet this guy's dad, get my recommendation, and get the hell out.

"My pleasure," I replied through gritted teeth. But as we rocked side-to-side, still so close together, I smelled the alcohol on his breath. So fucking gross.

I turned my head aside to avoid the smell. But my blonde, pretty-boy 18-year-old date who acted like he owned the world didn't like that.

"No no, look at me while we dance," he spat back. "Plus you're a lot prettier than I remember from our date."

Ugh. "Okay..."

His eyes started glancing down at my lips every couple seconds. I knew that look. Not because a boy's done that to me before, but because it's what I did with Kelly on the night of our fake date. I winced, and turned my head away again.

"I can't believe I'm actually into you," Bryce said in another terrible attempt at flattery.

I gulped. "Seriously. You *don't* have to be."

"I know it'd be a little faggy, but... Hey, I'd fuck you."

Fuck this. I'd had enough of his ridiculous, demeaning comments. I didn't want to be treated like an item. I'm taking space whether he likes it or not.

Tearing my body away from him, I ditched the dance floor.

It wasn't easy, but I maintained a look of sanity on my face as I strode past the other couples, catching many looks of confusion, but very few of concern.

I needed out. Out of the dance floor. Out of the ballroom. Out of the *night*. I ran into the women's restroom, praying I didn't encounter the transphobic lifeguards again. At the very least, I knew I was passable as a woman to the average GDCC member.

I stared at myself in the mirror, wanting to slap myself for even coming here tonight. How could I make this mistake? Dressing as a girl? I *knew* that all it ever did was fuck things up and make my life more difficult. And yet, here I am again tonight! Doing it all over again...

If the bathroom were empty, I'd have probably cried on the spot, staring at my beautiful but cursed reflection in the mirror. But tears would only cause more chaos. Ruined makeup never makes for a good introduction.

Fuck... I knew coming here tonight was a mistake. But I was so bought into the cause and necessity of relying on Bryce's father's connection, that turning back now would be an even bigger mistake. It was time to straighten up, walk back out there, and finish this night like the proper lady Bryce certainly *doesn't* deserve.

But exiting the bathroom provided no immediate relief. Because red in the face and suppressed tears in my eyes, I found myself running straight into another person. Suddenly face to face with who I *least* wanted to see me in this state.

Kelly.

20

"I'm sorry, I'm sorry," I said quickly, retreating while hiding my face. I didn't want him to see me. Certainly not like this.

"Andie, are you okay?" he asked, lunging toward me, knowing something must be wrong. "You look off."

I bravely turned toward him, hating that I had to address the fact that I was here as the guest of a member while he was stuck here working. In fact, he was carrying a tray full of napkin-wrapped silverware in case members wanted clean forks for their dessert.

And despite our vastly different nights, he looked fantastic. Handsome, put-together... everything a girl would want. And there *I* was, fresh off of crying from stress and actively shoveling my distress back inside my body.

"I'm okay, really. I'm here on a date. It's going really well."

Kelly looked at me, not fully believing my self-assuredness. "It *is*..."

"Yes," I answered as confidently as possible. "With Bryce Fox. I'm here with Bryce Fox. He's my date."

Still, Kelly looked skeptical. Not of my triple confirmation that Bryce was my date, but skeptical that everything was okay. "Look, Andie, I've been meaning to tell you something. I did a lot of thinking about the other night..."

The two of us weren't in the ballroom, but I knew that any second now Bryce could emerge from down the hall, spot me with Kelly, and *flip* out. And could I really blame him? Who wants to see their date talking to another man – even if he *is* straight.

"I'm very much in the middle of something, okay? If you have something to say, can you just... I dunno... text me or, like, *Trinity* tomorrow?"

Without waiting for his response, I scurried back to the ballroom with my head down, hoping to interact with as few people as possible. I probably looked as off as I felt.

"Andie, if something – *anything* – is wrong... Let me know. I'm here to help you."

Fuck that was sweet... A deep, genuine kindness I hadn't witnessed all night.

But of course, how do I respond? I stupidly refused to turn around and instead held up a thumbs-up to show him I heard him clearly.

I stumbled back into the hall like a messy, embarrassing idiot. Those who saw me probably thought I was drunk, like

Allie. Or hell, like *so* many people here. Just another drunk, rich girl living off daddy's money, here with her even richer date.

Everything felt blurry and fuzzy. I kept stumbling around, looking for Bryce. I felt horrible knowing that the same guy who's been calling me slurs all night and making me feel like shit – *that* was the guy I was looking for. To return right back to his side, so I could be his pretty, proper date. God I feel disgusting.

"Andie!" I heard someone shout. I realized it was Bryce, standing near the table where we ate. But he was with a man. I'd met so many people tonight – *too* many – but not this man. I think... I think this is his father.

He took a few steps toward me but instead of helping steady me, he gripped my arm. Aggressively hard.

"Time to meet my dad," he said through gritted teeth. "Be. Fucking. *Normal*."

Maybe it was his vague threat or just the adrenaline of knowing my moment had come, but I suddenly felt a lot better. My head was clear once again. I felt... *ready*.

"Mr. Fox, hello," I said, suddenly perked up, much to Bryce's surprise. "Such a pleasure to meet you."

The man was objectively dashing. And for someone in his mid to late 50s, he looked impressively youthful, but in a silver fox type of way. If he weren't the father of such a terrible son, I'd have garnered an immediate respect for him.

"Miss Miller, likewise," he reached out to shake my hand.

"Saffron," I corrected. "Andie Saffron. Trinity Miller is my aunt."

He raised an eyebrow, glaring at his son as if he gave faulty information. "So she is…"

Despite the awkward start, we made small talk for a minute or so. And somehow, I managed to come across charming. We shared laughs, traded a few observations and anecdotes… He was intimidating, sure, but appealing. It was obvious why he was so successful in the business world.

"Dad, I'm gonna grab dessert," Bryce interrupted in the middle of one of his father's stories.

Mr. Fox turned his head slowly, visibly annoyed. "Then go *grab* some. Don't just *tell* me."

As Bryce stepped away, I wasn't sure whether to chuckle at the expense of his son or just pretend I didn't see anything. I decided on the latter. But Mr. Fox watched his son walk away until he reached a healthy distance. Then, his tone suddenly changed from affable to business-like.

The man looked back at me, humorlessly. "I know what you are."

What? Only seconds had passed and Mr. Fox had become a starkly different person. "Uh, pardon me?"

"You're one of those transgenders. I knew something was up when my son was being all shifty about his lack of a date."

I couldn't believe what he was saying. I kept my head forward, but my eyes darted around, wondering if others were hearing what I was. "I'm sorry, should I…"

Mr. Fox held out his hand. "Oh no no no. I don't have a *problem* with you people. It's just… Well, my son's a bit of a dud, so I'm not particularly surprised. No offense, of course."

I *did* take offense, but hell, what was I supposed to do other than just stare blankly back at him?

"But he picked you as his date, and that's his decision. You're quite charming, Andie. And very beautiful for one of those transgenders."

I mumbled a little 'thank you', but immediately felt gross legitimizing a backhanded compliment like that.

Mr. Fox turned his head around again to check for the status of his son. He was in the act of piling dessert on his plate and would be back soon.

"I'll be brief. *Anyone* who can put up with my son I can hold admiration for. And if it's one of you people he wants... then so be it. I can get over it."

Bryce was now heading back to the table, plate full of food in his hands. The dizziness from before was returning, watching him approach.

"...So I feel it's important to offer you my resources as a gesture," Mr. Fox added quickly. "I hear you want to be a nurse. I have friends at hospitals all over the midwest. *Very good* friends. In time, as you continue dating my son, I'll make introductions. As you get to know him..."

Finally I chimed in. But much louder and more abrasive than I anticipated "As I *get to know* him?"

It was loud enough that Bryce heard. "Get to know who? Me?"

I sat there silent for a moment. Bryce, confused. His father, staring at me, waiting for an apology. When I didn't, Mr. Fox calmly clarified.

"I suppose everything's out in the air. I was just telling

Andie that as you two date, she will slowly earn the privileges of our family, right?"

Bryce stood there, bewildered. I glared at him, waiting for him to correct his father. He *knew* that wasn't the deal. He promised that *one* night as his date would get me a job. And yet...

He nodded. Like a spineless fool. "Mhmm. *As* we get to know each other, yes."

The time for peace and good behavior was over. Bryce had fucked me over one last time.

"You know what?" I said, shooting up from my seat and nearly tripping over my dress. I pointed my index finger straight to Bryce. "Fuck. YOU!"

For the first time all evening, his father looked shocked. But Mr. Fox needed his comeuppance too. "And you're just as gross as your fucking son!"

It was a cathartic but frighteningly unhinged fit of rage and frustration. But I no longer cared. I couldn't stand one more second being associated with such scummy, despicable people. The lies, the transphobia... everything.

Storming past the tables this time around, I didn't care who saw me. Because it wasn't just Bryce or his father. It was this club. I couldn't be here any more. I know it's not the fault of everyone, but a girl can only live without sympathy for so long before losing her goddamn mind.

The entire ballroom felt like a biohazard zone that required immediate evacuation. I needed to be as far away from here as possible. Even the ladies bathroom didn't feel secure enough as surely one of Mr. Fox's cronies could swoop in to ridicule me further. The club – my de facto second home for the entire summer – no longer felt safe to me.

I ran down the hallway in tears, deciding who, if *anyone*, I could dare ask for a hand. Bryce? Never again. Tara? Certainly too busy with the event. Kelly? Even with his offer, I knew I would somehow only hurt him again. Trinity? Does she even *want* me back in her home after so wholly disappointing her?

The parking lot felt like a horrible idea as Bryce and his father would most certainly search for me there. So I kept running down the hall until I found myself outside, ultimately deciding that my sanctuary within my home-away-from-home – the tennis courts – was my best bet.

It was silent when I arrived, unsurprisingly. I didn't have my keys on me, so there was no way to get inside. So instead, I plopped down on one of the many gold-painted benches right outside. Finally at peace, finally alone, I shoved my face into my hands and cried.

The release of tears felt both so relieving but also so damning. I thought of my wasted summer – how I came here to learn and to grow and all I did was waste my time playing dress up and tanking my relationships. Surely even with a passing grade on the NCLEX, with how powerful Mr. Fox is, he could blacklist me at every hospital in Chicago. Every hospital in the *midwest*, even.

I thought of Trinity and the beautiful relationship we'd developed was destroyed by my selfishness. Her pain from so many lost children was only exacerbated by my own disregard. And now I was added to the list.

And of course, Kelly too. The man who at first infuriated

me, but ultimately awakened who I was. He gave me so many chances to be a reasonable, normal friend and I let him down each step of the way.

So here I was – Cinderella, minutes before midnight. Her last night in a beautiful dress. But God, was I jealous of Cinderella because, even if she didn't *know* it when leaving the ball, she gets Prince Charming back and becomes the princess she so deserved to be. But me? I leave the ball and turn back into a pumpkin.

I sat there for a few more minutes, letting the tears fall down my face – *certainly* ruining my makeup. I figured I could get by waiting here a few hours for the party to end. And once everyone left, I could walk down to the guard gate and call an uber. A lonely but appropriate end to this night.

"Andie?"

My head perked up in fight-or-flight mode. The voice was coming from far down the way. But it was a woman's voice. A voice I recognized.

The woman, dressed in a beautiful emerald gown, was indeed someone I knew quite well. It was Janice.

She looked at me at first with shock, and then immediate concern. She shuffled over to me and plopped right down on the bench beside me, putting her arm on my shoulder.

"Oh, sweetie... Are you okay?"

I nodded, sniffling. It really was good to see her.

"You look beautiful," I said, to which she laughed.

"Not as beautiful as you!" she replied in good spirits. Say what you will about her, she can certainly lighten up a room. "It took me forever to find you. I was afraid you'd gone home."

I shook my head. "Just waiting for everyone to leave."

"Well that's nonsense! No girl deserves to take an uber home on the night of the ball."

I looked at her plainly. "Didn't you see what I did back there? How I screamed at Mr. Fox? And at Bryce?"

She gave a dismissive shrug. "I did... But knowing you, I'm sure you were in the right. Those guys are pricks."

"I'm sorry I didn't say hello. I didn't see you."

"Please, don't worry about it. My husband snagged us a table way on the other side. He insists the north side of the ballroom gets less chilly. But I know he's crazy."

I hung my head. It was nice to know *one* person here didn't hate my guts.

"Can I say something? Whatever the result of the night, do *not* let it spoil your future."

That was much easier said than done, but I appreciated the sentiment. "Heh... *Trust* me, I hope so too."

Janice kindly offered me a ride home on the spot. An offer which I tried to reject out of the desire not to ruin *her* night as well... But she wouldn't back down. So after doing a quick scan of the parking lot to make sure neither Bryce or his father were there, we rushed into the safety of her car.

Though Janice was certainly more modest-*acting* than Bryce, her car was an equally impressive Porsche 911. She quickly reminded me that this car was the choice of her *husband*, and not her. I guess her husband really lives for the glitz and the glamor like the rest of the GDCC folks.

On the ride home, Janice kindly kept the conversation light and on anything *other* than the dance. It took her almost ten minutes, but she even got me to laugh. Despite the heavy circumstances, I felt a lot better talking to her.

We pulled up to my house where, understandably, the lights in the window were out. Trinity was asleep. The single porch light was the one thing illuminating up my soon to be former home here on Lumber Lane.

I told Janice to drop me off at the end of the driveway so as not to wake Trinity. She reached over to the passenger's seat to give me an ill-positioned, sweet hug.

"Don't let tonight get you down, okay sweetie?"

"I'll try," I answered gloomily, though admittedly in the best mood I'd been in all night.

I got out and Janice began to drive away. Though she only got five feet before rolling down her window again.

"I'm sorry, I *know* this is none of my business, but... Maybe you give that boy another chance."

What?

"Excuse me?" I said, floored. "You want me to give *Bryce* another chance?"

"No no no," Janice clarified, terrified by my misunderstanding. "The *first* boy."

What was she talking about...

"Janice, I only went on a date with Bryce."

She rubbed the bridge of her nose, trying to explain herself. "*No.* That boy who was a server tonight. The one who's also a lifeguard."

Again... *What?*

Janice looked at me funny. "Well, damn, sorry if I read you wrong... But he clearly wants *you* back."

Her lack of clarity was driving me insane. "JANICE. WHAT ARE YOU TALKING ABOUT?"

"That boy... Kelly, I think is his name. Each time I leave our lessons, I catch him hanging around outside – *super* nervous and waiting for you to come outside. Andie, last time he even had flowers."

21

Umm... *WHAT* did she just say?

"Janice, we can't be talking about the same guy. Because if you are... he's *not* into me. He's... he's just *NOT*."

Janice smirked a little. "Ehh... I'm pretty sure it's the same guy. *Super* cute, short brunette hair? Got those *really* broad swimmer shoulders. He was a server tonight!"

Jesus... She *can't* be talking about Kelly... But then again, it's his exact description. I had a million questions for her, but right as I was about to rattle off, she got a phone call.

"Hi Honey... Yeah, I'm on my way back. My friend needed a ride home real bad. Heading back now!" Janice hung up the phone. "Andie, I really have to go."

"Janice! You can't just leave me like *this*–"

She chuckled. "Oh, so *now* you're into this boy? Well, let's book another lesson and we'll talk about it then, 'kay?"

Without another word, Janice sped away down the street.

What else can I say but that I'm dumbstruck. *Kelly* – the boy who'd been right there the whole time – was actually interested in me? The teasing, the discomfort... Was it not an aversion, but rather an attraction?

This news made me feel woozy again, so I stumbled down the driveway back towards the house. Still not wishing to wake up Trinity and disturb the still night, I took a moment to sit and reflect on her front porch, looking out toward the unlit street.

There's no possible way to broach the subject with Kelly. He was hard at work, safely away from me. So maybe it's for the best. Frankly it's been such a long night. I could use the opportunity to sleep on it and not be irrational.

But just as I made up my mind to go to bed, I noticed the street, way out in front, light up. A car was coming, and *fast*. The violent, revving of an engine made me think it had to be Janice speeding back to tell me something. Or to take me back to the club, for some reason.

I stood up to get a better view as I saw a car turn into the driveway. It was so dark, I couldn't tell who it was, but *God* were they driving fast. Fast, and definitely without respect for the neighbors or Trinity.

As the car got closer I was able to recognize bits of the car reflecting off the porch light. And no, it wasn't Janice's car. It was a black Ferrari.

My curiosity quickly turned to fear as the spaceship-like car door lifted open and out hopped Bryce from the driver's seat. His hair was messy and eyes were fiery.

"You FUCKING bitch!" he screamed ferociously.

I stood there, paralyzed, unable to say anything as he stormed onto the lawn aching to give me a piece of his mind.

"Where the FUCK do you get off pulling a stunt like that in front of my dad?" he yelled again, beckoning me to come off the porch. But again, I simply couldn't move.

"Bryce, you need to go home. You're drunk," I squeaked out, not sure what to say.

"No no no, you're gonna fucking come down here, get in my car, and apologize to my dad. RIGHT. NOW."

The boy was blind with rage. Even his thin, wispy frame looked horrifying.

For some reason, my paralysis momentarily ceased and I was able to think straight. I needed to get inside to safety. So I made a quick move down the long porch toward the front door.

But Bryce didn't like that, and he started stomping up to the porch. "Don't you *fucking* go inside you fucking tranny..."

I nervously dug around my purse for the house keys. Whether I'd forgotten them or I was too petrified to properly search, they couldn't be summoned. I frantically looked around for backup options. Do I run right past him? Do I jump down from this porch and make a break for it? Or shuffle into the backyard to hide?

"Trinity!!" I banged on the door in desperation.

I watched as Bryce slowly made his way toward the porch. Until he suddenly stopped.

The street illuminated again with the light of a *second* car. And the sound of a *second* revving engine. This time of a *non*-sports car.

"Who the fuck did you call??" Bryce shouted, suddenly concerned. "Cops aren't that fast."

The incoming car whipped into the driveway, speeding before screeching to a halt and nearly colliding with the parked Ferrari.

But it wasn't the cops. And it wasn't Janice... It was *Kelly*.

"Kelly! Stop him!"

Without missing a beat or saying a word, Kelly leaped out of his car and sprinted right toward Bryce.

"What, is this your boyfriend or someth–" Bryce questioned, only to get steamrolled onto the lawn from a full-speed Kelly.

"WHAT THE FUCK!" Bryce screamed out in fear, helplessly pinned to the grass by the much stronger man.

I watched nervously from the porch as Kelly shoved the back of Bryce's head into the dirt, securing him down, but clearly wanting nothing more than to pummel him to pieces.

"Get the fuck away from her!" Kelly boomed.

"Fuck, alright, alright!" Bryce spat out, his mouth full of dirt and deeply in pain from Kelly's forceful tackle.

Kelly remained on top of Bryce for a moment, eyeing him like prey.

"Ow! Owowow! I wasn't gonna do anything... *Jesus!*" Bryce bellowed, squirming beneath Kelly's size like a mouse caught in a trap.

"Kelly, it's fine. Let him go." I directed him, who cautiously let Bryce up from the ground.

"Get in the car..." Kelly commanded Bryce.

Bryce shot him a wicked grin, his mouth still bleeding from the impact.

"Nah," Bryce retorted. "Not like this."

Then with blazing speed, Bryce sucker-punched Kelly in the jaw, knocking him to the ground. With Kelly sufficiently stunned, Bryce took the chance to kick Kelly in the stomach, once, twice, and three times, causing him to scream out in pain.

Bryce cackled, much preferring this side of the fight. But just before his fourth kick, Kelly grabbed his leg and yanked *Bryce* to the ground with a violent thud.

I shrieked from the porch with a mix of fear and aggression as I watched the two boys' grudge match on the ground – Kelly gaining the advantage with his strength, then Bryce stealing it right back with his speed. I had no idea if running onto the lawn to fight with Kelly would help or only make things worse.

But a decision was unnecessary because only a moment later, the front door burst open from behind me. Storming right beside my frozen body, armed with a handgun and a look of parental rage, was Trinity.

Both boys turned their heads and swiftly halted their battle upon spotting my gun-wielding aunt perched on the porch.

"Get off the ground!" she commanded. The boys did as told.

"*You,*" Trinity waved the gun at Bryce. "Get into that car of yours, turn around, and NEVER come back.."

Bryce, for the first time all night, looked like he was an inch tall. His eyes were welling up with tears – part from the pain and part from the fear.

"B-but..." he stammered. "His car is block–"

Trinity cocked the gun, which made Bryce immediately

shut up. He sprinted to his car, closed the door, and carefully turned around on the lawn, snaking past Kelly's car. We watched his car crawl toward the road and then sped off into the night.

Kelly was now alone on the lawn still panting from the fight. I felt close to passing out from anxiety, terror, and stress of the night. But Trinity? She looked weirdly content.

"Can't do *that* shit with a broken body, huh?" she smirked, twirling her handgun. "Come on, let's clean up inside."

NEITHER KELLY nor I said much as we waited patiently in the dimly lit living room. Kelly on the couch, me seated in a chair across from him.

We looked and felt like natural disaster victims, physically and emotionally wounded, wrapped up in blankets, and being served hot tea to calm our nerves. I was still processing all the crazy, chaotic moments of the night. But at the very least I knew we were home safe with Trinity.

"And here's yours, Kelly," Trinity offered him a warm mug which he gladly accepted. She took a seat next to Kelly and kindly placed her hand on his shoulder. He winced in pain just a bit.

"So..." she continued, sitting up properly in her fuzzy pink robe. "I gave the police a heads up to look for a drunk driver in a black Ferrari out on the road. But turns out a cop was already heading over after someone reported the shouting from my lawn. They pulled him over just a minute down the road."

At least a small amount of justice was served. Though I think we all felt relieved knowing Bryce couldn't hurt anyone else tonight.

Trinity glimpsed at the clock, gasping at the time. "Jeez! I didn't realize how late it'd gotten. As much as I'd love to unpack more of the night, I think I'll be more attentive in the morning."

While I had a million and one things still to share with Trinity, I appreciated that she could both take care of business while still taking care of herself. As I've said before, she's the most impressive lady I know.

"Andie, you can see Kelly out if he wishes. Or Kelly, if you want to stay the night, I have sheets for the couch in the linen closet. Andie can help you with that."

We smiled gratefully and wished Trinity goodnight as she disappeared down the hall, shutting her bedroom door.

Out of all the scary things tonight, I somehow found myself most nervous right now, alone with Kelly. Not our first time *alone*, but the first time since everything I knew about him changed.

"You're giving me a weird look," he began, touching his face. "Am I bleeding?"

"No. Trinity cleaned it up. I'm just looking at you."

He sighed, thinking for a moment. "You know, *you* should've been the one to clean up my face, being a nurse and all."

I smiled, chuckling. "Am I not allowed to be off duty? After everything I went through tonight, you expect me to work?"

"If you're as good as you say you are, yeah, I do!"

Kelly looked absolutely exhausted, but still managed to smile at me. Just like that, we were bickering again. It was so light and playful, I think we both needed it. An escape from the heaviness of the last few hours. But still, I couldn't just ignore what he gave to me tonight.

"You really came in clutch there, you know? And speeding down the driveway? *Super* badass."

"I felt like Vin Diesel in those shitty Fast and Furious movies. I can't believe my car didn't fall apart."

We laughed. It's no Ferrari, that's for sure.

I gazed at the beaten-down, dinged-up man. "How did you know I was in trouble?" I asked. "I didn't see you in the ballroom."

He shook his head. "I wasn't. But I wish I was or I would've just beat the shit out of him then and there. Save the gas money, you know?"

Heh. Always the practical one...

Kelly continued. "But a coworker later told me things got heated between you two, that you screamed at him and ran out of the clubhouse. Nobody knew where you went. I was about to text you, but my phone was dead. Then I saw Bryce fighting with his father in the hallway. It looked messy, and Bryce looked demonic. And when I saw him leave for his car–"

"Your instincts were right," I said, cutting him off and not needing to relive the rest. "Thank you."

"Don't mention it," he said, dabbing a cut on his lip. "But hey, can we talk about Trinity's *gun*?? I never took her for that type."

"Oh my god, me neither!" I exclaimed, then peered affectionately down the hall. "But she's a strong, independent woman. What can I say?"

Kelly gazed into my eyes. "So are you," he said with a bit more seriousness.

His tone made my heart skip a beat. "Well, I'm still—"

"Look, uh, Andie... There's some stuff I've been meaning to tell you. Stuff that's, like, *way* overdue."

"I have an idea," I answered, holding eye contact . "If I can guess it, can I win something?"

Kelly smirked. "Mmm... I don't think you'll be able to guess it."

"Well, it took a while but now I'm *so* confident, I bet I can guess it without even saying a word."

He raised an eyebrow, not sure what I meant. Ugh, *boys*.

I got up from my chair and confidently sat down next to him, staring him in the eyes. "Like th–"

But before I could finish, Kelly leaned in for a kiss of his own. And not just any kiss. A long, passionate, *deeply* romantic kiss. The kind that fills your entire body with a rush of euphoric warmth.

"Beat you to it," he said, finally releasing his lips.

Goddamn did this boy have an effect on me. I wanted him just as much as he wanted me.

"Take me upstairs. There are some things I've been meaning to try with you *off*-camera."

22

My night with Kelly was everything I could've dreamed of and more. While admittedly neither of us *totally* knew what we were doing, we channeled our pent-up passion and adrenaline into a beautiful exploration of each other's bodies. Yes, I *did* finally get to see him naked in real life and yes, it *was* glorious.

At times the night felt awkward and wasn't always easy, but the things that man did to my delicate little body — using his hands, tongue, and cock alike – made me feel like the woman I set out to be that night. And the chance to be gently held by him as I drifted off to sleep was the cherry on top.

I feared waking up the following morning that I'd be drowning in regret. That I, once more, had somehow disappointed Kelly, Trinity, or another close person in my life by pursuing my femininity. But as my eyes crept open to the morning light in my bedroom, spooned by Kelly's large, warm body, I felt at ease – both with myself and with my decisions. My trauma from last night's ball would be dealt with eventually... but not now. Anytime but now. I wanted to live *in* the now, soaking in the bliss of this perfect moment.

Eventually I flipped over and kissed Kelly on the nose to wake him up. Turns out we'd stayed like that the entire night, cuddling close – Kelly in his boxers, me in my panties. It was chilly getting out of bed, so I threw on one of the boyish hoodies I'd worn several times in the past week. In reality it was mine, but in my mind I pretended I was borrowing Kelly's.

Kelly couldn't stay here forever and I'm sure his absence had already concerned his parents – assuming they even *care* where he goes. Thus began the inevitable walk of shame.

We tried to be as quiet as possible to not wake Trinity or suggest that Kelly stayed the night in my room. But as I snuck him downstairs to the front door, Trinity startled us from behind wearing the same fuzzy pink robe and holding a half-finished cup of coffee.

"Fun night?" she said to both of us, turning redder than ever before.

"Good morning," I squeaked out, still wearing my girls' robe. Kelly was dressed haphazardly in last night's work uniform.

Trinity, the darling she is, graciously refrained from teasing Kelly and let us say our goodbyes in private at the front door. One last sweet kiss on the lips, and Kelly was on his way.

"Well, well, well..." Trinity jeered playfully as I returned to the kitchen.

"I figured I couldn't hide it for long..."

"Oh *that?*" she gestured upstairs. "I don't wanna hear one second about what you two kids did up there. I mean, I'm *happy* for you, but... I'm still your aunt."

We laughed, both grateful I didn't need to divulge anything too personal. But still, Trinity wanted me to sit down with her and give a little more detail on the last night. Both the wonderful and the painful.

We chatted for nearly an hour. What began as a recap of the night soon turned into a venting session, which *then* turned into a confessional. A real heart-to-heart. Something that was long overdue between the two of us.

"Look, if I knew about your past... And all those horrible things Vince–"

She held up her hand. "It's in the past. And honestly, that's the best thing about it. I have *such* a great life now. And *fuck* if it's been nice to be able to share it with someone for once, no matter the relationship. Even if it *is* just for the summer..."

I hung my head, not wanting to watch her cry because if *she* did, I would too.

"I mean... regardless of where I end up... you'll always have a niece."

Her head lifted up, excited but skeptical. "Wait, *Anderson...* You mean..."

I nodded. "I think I decided sometime last night. This life I've got ahead of me... It's too scary and complicated on its own without having to live as someone I'm not. So if it's okay with you, I'd like to start living as Andie."

Trinity shot up from her seat, ecstatic and in tears. At this point it was unavoidable, and I lost all control too. Trinity lunged across the room and held me close with the warm, loving hug of an aunt.

Maybe she didn't find her forever *daughter*, but she found the next best thing.

IT TOOK ONLY a week for Old Buffalo's vibe to completely change from summer escape back into its everyday, small town feel. The homes on Lumber Lane and other lakeside properties rented by wealthy Chicagoans were returned to their owners as the Chicagoans returned to the city. And the tourist-reliant summer businesses like boating, fishing, and community event-planning left with them.

The summer was drawing to a close and everybody could feel it. Myself included, as I was fast-approaching my move-out date, returning to Chicago to take my test, find a job, and restart my life as Andie.

The prospect of starting anew had replaced one terror with another. No longer was I afraid of finding an apartment, passing the test, and getting a job. Well, maybe *that's* not true. I still feared those things. But the new lingering concern was my seemingly insurmountable challenge of beginning the long, arduous transition into the woman I knew I had to be. With my looks and support system, I'd have it far easier than so many others do – but that didn't mean it'd be all sunshine and roses. Not even close.

But before I could even *think* about that, I wanted to honor my personal pledge to keep living in the moment and enjoy my final two weeks as an Old Buffalonian.

ONCE THE DUST finally settled from all the GDCC ball drama, Trinity planned to march right into the club membership office to terminate her membership, effective immediately.

Now believe me, I *insisted* it wasn't necessary and that my opinions on certain club members should have no bearing on her enjoyment of the facilities. But Trinity wholeheartedly disagreed. To her, the club she belongs to is an extension of herself and her values. And in her eyes, the time she spent putting up with shifty rich folks had gone on for far too long. The incident with Bryce and his father was simply the straw that broke the camel's back.

As for my employment, I planned to quit only a few weeks later, so Tara graciously allowed me to leave a couple weeks early on good terms.

Speaking of which, Tara was *distraught* upon learning what went down with Bryce. She called me the very next day after Trinity yelled at her for 'letting the fox into the hen house' – no pun intended. While I would've loved to have *not* gone through the trauma of an aggressive, drunk transphobe like Bryce, I found it unfair to pin any of this on Tara. Sure, she whiffed on a setup. But she was only trying to help me out. A gesture which I, at the time – and *still* today – deeply appreciated.

Kelly ended up quitting his lifeguard position too. Tara, of course, harbored no ill will, but it sucked knowing Kelly's reputation among the club members would almost certainly be ruined. It's only a matter of time until inevitably false rumors spread from the Fox camp, suggesting he went rogue and beat up a member's son... or something bullshit like that. Still, his exit from Golden Dunes allowed him the opportunity to take some space and figure out what he truly wants to pursue.

While I had no bearing on his *long* term future, I'm happy to say I've been very much part of Kelly's *short* term plans. 'Dating' might be the wrong word, but over the past week, Kelly and I have seen each other nearly every day. The rush of our first hookup was too much to ignore. All it took was that first night to get us hooked on each other.

It all had a temporary, exploratory air to it though. We confessed to our slow-burn, secret crushes on *each other*, but that didn't mean Kelly was ready to come out to his parents. Partly because he didn't even *have* a label yet. 'Pansexual', to him, was the closest term he could find and what he's been saying to me, Trinity, and a select few others for the time being.

We'd developed a nice routine in such a short time. He works odd jobs during the day while I study. Then at night, he comes over to hang out with me and Trinity. And once Trinity goes to bed, we have our alone time up in my room. Simple and perfect.

My time with Kelly was beautiful but fleeting. My move was fast approaching, and I tried not to dwell on it. Doing so only made me more sad.

"Ooh! What about this one?" Trinity enthusiastically pointed to a page on her laptop.

"Ugh, alright..." I groaned, reluctantly rising from the couch as she called from the kitchen. This was like the ninth time in 15 minutes she'd made me walk over.

Nearly two weeks removed from her bombastic exit from Golden Dunes, Trinity was growing extremely antsy without a proper social or athletic outlet. In other words, she desperately wanted another country club.

"'The Harris Club'," she read aloud, scrolling around the club's glitzy website. "And it's only an hour-fifteen away!"

"Hard to beat the proximity of Golden Dunes..." I muttered, still a little regretful that *I* was essentially her whole reason for leaving.

"Nope. I told you, I'm never going back. Those people can fuck off. I'm gonna find one with kind, outgoing, *engaging* members. A place where me *and* you can feel welcome."

Classic, stubborn Trinity.

"Trinity, I'm literally out of here..." I thought for a moment, counting the days. "...*this* Saturday. That's three days! My opinion should mean nothing."

"Your opinion means *everything!* Just because you're moving back to Chicago doesn't mean you won't visit. I expect you to be here at *least* once a month."

We've had a version of this conversation many times already. "I know, I know, I'll *try*..."

Leaving Kelly, leaving Trinity... hell, the thought of leaving *Old Buffalo* put me in a sour mood. For a summer trip that was only meant as a pit stop, it's undeniable the amount of growth I experienced in such a short few months. Not only did my gender and sexuality awaken, but my views on family, friends, and community matured. Life can't simply be 'do X to get Y'. Your experiences should matter, and they should matter *in* the moment. Not everything will, or *should*, be flowery all the time. But isn't that the beauty of it? The ups and downs? The maturity we get from these experiences? I think too many people forget that.

I INSISTED Trinity create no fanfare or anything beyond a simple, home cooked meal for the two of us on my final night as an Old Buffalo resident. Her tendency to go over-the-top was appreciated, but I knew anything too much would only make me miss this place more.

Kelly, however, I *did* allow to take me on a proper dinner date the night before – but maybe a *wee* bit of that was me wanting to be pampered one last time before our iffy, 'what's our status', long-distance fling begins. It was far too soon to put a label on us, and both of us respected that fact. I didn't think it was the last night I'd ever see him, but it was unfortunately the last time under these carefree circumstances.

I genuinely hate goodbyes, so the thought of a banner, a cake, or any of that crap to send me off felt unnecessary. 'So long for *now*' was much preferred. So after some tense negotiations with Trinity, we agreed on a home cooked meal for dinner and a final trip to MooMoo's for ice cream before coming back home for a girls' movie night. To me, this couldn't be more perfect.

She really brought her A-Game too, preparing a delicious risotto, pairing it with grilled asparagus and a fabulous cabernet. We feasted like queens while we chatted at the table.

"Ready for ice cream?" Trinity later asked, checking her phone for the time.

Dinner didn't end too long ago and I still felt quite stuffed. "Eh, a little early, right?"

"Oh *c'mon*, I'm hungry again! The lines are always long anyway. You'll get hungrier in the car, I promise."

Trinity seemed a tad off all night, so I let her have her way. Besides, it was less *about* the ice cream and more about the time spent with her. I was happy to oblige.

"And I should add... I do have *one* little surprise for you..."

My eyes nearly rolled back in my head. "Ugh! *Trinity*! I said no surprises!"

"Ohhh shut up. I'm allowed to give you *one* surprise," she explained as she ran off to the front closet to fetch something. She returned holding some kind of outfit in her arms.

"I know you're not filming for Princess Trinity anymore, but you were nonetheless sent this dress from a favorite brand. I think you should wear it to ice cream."

The dress she held in her hands was hands down one of the cutest little dresses I'd seen to date. It was a light green floral cami dress with an adorable string to tie in the front. Simple, elegant, and very much my style.

"*Okay...* I accept your *one* surprise." I said, not-so-reluctantly giving in. "But only because it's literally my perfect kind of dress."

I ran upstairs to change as Trinity called from downstairs.

"And put that white bow in your hair too! I might want to take a picture of you on your last day, okay?"

Jeeeez, Trinity. Enough with the demands! But she's right again – as always. The bow would pair perfectly.

With my hair done up and my new dress on, we finally hopped into Trinity's car – an idea I was still getting used to, as she'd only *recently* been medically cleared to drive. We were off to MooMoo's for my final farewell.

The evening ride down Lumber Lane and onto Red Arrow Highway was simply magical. The sky was a beautiful mix of orange and pink as I watched in real time golden hour come upon us. God this was beautiful... If part of this ice cream trip was to make me miss this town even more, then mission accomplished.

MooMoo's was only a quick drive away and, just as predicted, there was a *massive* line out front. Dozens and dozens of people packed like cattle beneath the giant cartoon cow mascot, eagerly awaiting their ice cream.

But Trinity didn't pull into the parking lot. In fact, she sped right past it.

"Oh, uh, back there," I reminded her, assuming she'd spaced out. "You missed MooMoo's!"

Trinity took a deep breath. "Okay *please* don't be mad at me. I know I said no more surprises... But I have a *particularly* special one for you. And we're headed there right now."

23

I let out the *most* aggressive groan. Of course Trinity had another trick up her sleeve. Of *course.*

"Am I the biggest idiot for thinking you were really planning nothing but dinner and ice cream for my final day?"

Trinity was giggling uncontrollably at my reaction. "Yeah, you kinda are. I like spoiling my niece, so spoil my niece, I shall!"

I felt like a victim in the sweetest kidnapping scheme imaginable. Fooled and whisked away by my loving aunt for one final Old Buffalo surprise.

Or maybe not even Old Buffalo, because we kept driving down Red Arrow Highway. Far away. At least another 20 minutes.

"Are we *there* yet?" I teased in my kiddiest voice. Soon enough Trinity turned off the highway, down a side road, eventually passing a modest welcome sign labeled 'Baskerville.'

"Baskerville…" I read aloud the sign we passed. "I feel like I've heard before."

Trinity shrugged and smiled as she led us deeper into the town. By the looks of the homes, Baskerville was far more rural and *way* less touristy than Old Buffalo. The houses were nice but small, but far off the main road and each a healthy distance from the next. There's a lot more land when you're not constrained by a lake.

Still, why the hell was she taking me out here?

We drove another few minutes before finally reaching our destination. Trinity's Prius drifted to a slow stop on the street, down from a modern country home on a huge plot of land. It was now dusk, and the rapidly darkening sky loomed vast and large over the acres of mostly untouched, undeveloped dirt… with *one* strange outlier: the beginnings of a construction site on the east side of the home.

"Who lives here?" I asked Trinity, though was ignored as she parked and left the car.

"Just trust me. Come on!"

I cautiously followed her down the long driveway toward the home. Why we had to park on the street I didn't know, but Trinity didn't even bother going to the front door of the quaint, barn-like home. She walked straight toward the construction, and the closer we got, the clearer – but also more confusing – things became.

Paved asphalt… bit of chain-link fence… fluorescent flood lights…

"Is this… a *tennis* court?" I asked.

It certainly looked like one. And it was nearly finished. I hesitated joining Trinity on the court as I had *no* idea whose house this even was. This was all so weird and her lack of answers was really starting to annoy me.

"Trinity *WHAT* is going–" I began, but was cut off by the loud click and hum of the floodlights turning on, illuminating the tennis court.

"Trinity! I said to meet me at the front door!" a voice shouted out. A voice I'd become quite familiar with these past few months.

Emerging from the side door of the modest home was none other than Janice.

"Janice! I'm so sorry!" I shouted out almost instinctively. I'm not sure why, but I felt embarrassed to be seen like this around her. Not in my work uniform, a tennis dress, or anything proper – particularly while intruding on her property.

"Were you really gonna leave without saying goodbye?" she called out. "I know we texted, but I decided that simply won't do."

I turned toward Trinity, confused why we'd just crashed a random Saturday evening at Janice's home in the middle of nowhere.

"I... I'm sorry," I stuttered. "I've just been a little busy with packing and studying and..."

"Andie," Janice interrupted my spiral. "I'm *kidding*. But I did want to surprise you with something tonight."

I stared into the blinding lights of the half-constructed tennis court. "Well clearly, you're carrying on with tennis."

Janice nodded. "Because of you, yeah! But that's not the main surprise. This is just a little splurge I insisted on after leaving Golden Dunes. I thought you'd like to see it."

She left too? Damn, it seems everyone's ditching that place.

"I'm sorry you felt the need to leave. Will your husband be–"

"Eh, he'll be fine. Golf's everywhere. But good people aren't." Janice took a few steps closer to me as Trinity watched from afar. "But look, Andie, I'll be straight with you. We brought you out here tonight because I want to offer you a job."

I stared at Janice, her blonde bob cut shining under the fluorescent lights of her new tennis court.

"I don't think you understand... Look, I *loved* teaching you tennis. But I'm no *profess*–"

"No, Andie. A job as a nurse. At my hospital."

What?

Her hospital? *What??*

I immediately turned to Trinity and watched a sneaky little grin grow on her face.

"...*second* surprise!" she said softly.

The smiling ladies seemed to enjoy my frazzled lack of comprehension. "Janice, *what* are you talking about? You're a *receptionist*, right?"

"That's true, I take shifts at reception because I *like* working at reception. I do it because I get to meet and connect with all sorts of new people. People like you, Andie. But my husband and I own the hospital. And we have for almost 30 years."

I started feeling genuinely woozy from the information overload, and I could tell Trinity got a huge kick out of it.

Janice kept explaining. "I've never been one to flaunt wealth. In fact, I kinda hate it, and it's an argument I have with my husband frequently. That stupid car I drove you home in... that was a compromise. We live in a modest home, have a modest day-to-day... It's a better way to live life, trust me."

I pointed to the ongoing construction. "And the tennis court?"

"Okay, *sometimes* I'll splurge," Janice conceded. "Andie, the point is I've been teetering for years on whether to open up a new non-profit clinic in Old Buffalo, and I'm not sure why, but since meeting you, I finally got the motivation to just freakin' DO it. So here I am, staffing up. It's not the glitz and the glam you'd find at Golden Dunes or in Chicago... but if you're interested, you're first on my list."

Everything was happening so fast. Trinity's surprise, Janice's reveal, now a *job* offer?

"I... I haven't even taken the boards yet."

Trinity scoffed. "Andie, you've been studying for *months*! You're obviously going to pass."

She's right... I'm more prepared for this than anything.

Janice took my hand and led me over to a bench just off the court. "I'm sorry to throw this all on you so abruptly. I know it's a massive decision. But it took me far too long to realize the importance of finding people you care about in life – who *also* care about *you* – and sticking with them. I watched you all summer grow as an instructor, as a friend... as a *human*. And now I want to help you grow as a nurse."

I looked back and forth between these two incredible women. "Does Kelly know about this?"

"I do."

Suddenly, Kelly emerged from the side door with a big grin on his face and holding flowers.

"Oh my god..." I blushed, embarrassed he'd been watching this whole thing. "*Stop* it..."

He sauntered up to me, looking all hunky under the night-time fluorescent light. "I never had the courage to give you those flowers outside the Golden Dunes courts, so I figured I'd do it tonight."

Again, I looked over to Trinity.

"...*third* surprise!" she said sheepishly.

There I stood, next to three individuals who'd made an extraordinary impact on my life this summer. People who showed kindness when it was needed most and never thought of themselves first. But most of all, these were people who were invested in me as a person – in me as a *woman*.

"I had to park *way* down the road so you wouldn't notice my car. That was a smart call from Janice." Kelly added. Janice mimed tipping her cap.

A tear trickled down from my eye. The love and warmth I felt was overwhelming gazing at these three incredible humans, all together under the beautiful, darkening Michigan sky. You know, I think I've been thinking about this wrong the whole time. There's a balance that must be struck between living in the moment and looking ahead to the future. *Both* are extremely important. But above all, happiness should be what wins the day. And I honestly couldn't think of a place I'm happier than in Old Buffalo.

It was time for a leap of faith. I looked squarely back at Janice, who was tearing up from the weight of the moment.

"Alright then. When do I start?"

THE END

ABOUT THE AUTHOR

Jennifer Sweet is a Midwest-born, West Coast-based author who passionately pens novels and novellas about boys finding their feminine sides -- anywhere from the sweet and innocent to the steamy and seductive.

Visit her website and sign up for her newsletter for the latest updates on upcoming books.

www.jennifersweetbooks.com

www.jennifersweetbooks.com/newsletter

ALSO BY JENNIFER SWEET

Dresses from Diana: A Gradual Feminization Story

You'll Fit Right In: A Gradual Feminization Story

Anthony's Influence: A Steamy, Gender-Bending Romance

In Rotation: A Gradual Feminization Story

Just Let Me Do Your Hair: A Gradual Feminization Story

Misscast: A Gradual Feminization Story

You're Beautiful: A Coming-of-Age Gender Discovery Tale

A Girl For Halloween: A Slow and Sweet Gender Realization Story

...and many more to come.

Printed in Great Britain
by Amazon

41532283R00148